MY NEW LIFE

Ron Molen

Signature Books   Salt Lake City
1 9 9 6

t o   S t e v e n

Cover painting by Norma L. Molen; "Summer Trees"
(detail); 16" x 11"; 1996; oil on canvas
Cover design by Lee Molen

∞ *My New Life* was printed on acid-free paper and was
composed, printed and bound in the United States.

00   99   98   97   96   6   5   4   3   2   1

Library of Congress Cataloging-in-Publication Data
Molen, Ronald L.
     My new life / by Ron Molen.
          p.   cm.
     ISBN 1-56085-073-6
     I. Title.
     PS3563.03955M9 1996
     813' .54—dc20   96-14254
                                            CIP

O   N   E

The Saturday after the last day of school was warm, muggy; storm clouds grayed the sky. I wandered down the alley behind my house following faint shouts that came from the vacant lot, a forest of giant poplars filled with snakes and spiders. The voices grew louder, more distinct. It was impossible to see through the wall of weeds, so I clawed my way in. Nettles cut my legs, a swarm of mosquitoes attacked, soon I was sweating. I found then followed a path of fresh crushed weeds that smelled sweet, and passed under vine-strangled apple trees buried in the forest darkness. When I entered a clearing, I saw a bunch of dirty, sweaty guys my age running back and forth building weed huts. They screamed at each other. Laughed. Cussed. An ugly one-eyed dog trotted up sniffing and snarling. Otherwise no one noticed me. I felt out of place.

Suddenly an older guy stepped forward. "I'm Grumble," he said, then pointed to a guy about my height with a belly round as a beach ball. "And this is Digger."

"Hi," said Digger. He was eight, a year older than I.

Grumble was probably ten.

I had seen them from a distance at school, but had never played with them. Grumble was six inches taller than everyone else. He acted like the leader, marching around shouting orders. Not that anyone paid attention, but that didn't bother him. I was fascinated. Here I was in a new world of sweaty guys and panting hounds, feeling a powerful connection to some long-forgotten time.

"What's your name?" Grumble said.

"Tom Bradshaw."

"You can't go by that," he said. He looked me over. "We'll call you Wart."

"That's good," Digger said. They both laughed, and their eyes let me know I was to do the same. Grumble told me to work with Digger on a hut that looked like all the others except it was larger and almost finished. The design was simple. Weeds were flattened in a round area, then surrounding grass was bent inward and tied together at the center. Cut weeds were then heaped on top. A thatched igloo. Inside the oldest hut, the rank air and mosquitoes were more than you could stand. It was first used as a latrine, but the hounds took it over and no effort was made to win it back.

Grumble finally called out, "It's time for a meeting." No one responded. "Come on, you guys."

"We're not done yet," Digger snapped.

"Doesn't matter!" Grumble shouted.

"What do we need a meeting for?" a smaller guy

said. He wore his dad's straw hat and was twice as dirty as Digger.

Grumble stepped up and gave him a shove. "Move it," he said, then grabbed Digger by the arm.

"All right," Digger said.

Someone pushed me, and I shoved the guy ahead. Soon we were sitting in a circle at our leader's feet.

Grumble scratched his hip, waiting. He wanted to be sure everyone was listening. Finally, he touched my shoulder. "This is Wart," he said. "He's working with Digger." I looked around, but no one cared.

Grumble pointed to the huts. "They look okay." He nodded and smiled. "With a little more work they could be nifty." His smile faded as he set his jaw and stretched to full height. "And we're not going to let those bastards from across the tracks tear them down."

"Who are they?" I blurted out. Everyone turned to me and my face grew hot.

Grumble stared in my direction, then at the rest in the circle. "There's a gang from across the tracks," he said. "They're the meanest guys you've ever seen. See this scar?" He held out his arm. "One of 'em bit me." I couldn't see a thing, yet he convinced me. The more he talked, the more excited we became.

In no time he whipped us into a frenzy and only stopped when Digger howled, "What can we do?"

Grumble smiled with the confidence of a healer. "Build a fire," he said. "A big fire." His black eyes narrowed as he bit his lip. "They're afraid of fire. That's our only hope."

We looked at each other.

Grumble pulled a handful of matches from his torn shirt pocket and held them high for everyone to see. "We must gather wood!" he shouted. "Bring all the wood you can find. And Digger, you and Wart run and get some papers. All you can carry."

Everyone scattered in different directions. Even the dogs raced back and forth, sensing something momentous was in the wind.

"Come on," Digger said. "Where do you live?"

"Across the alley."

"Have any newspapers?"

"In the basement," I said.

"Good, my house is too far away."

We took off running down the path, and his ugly, one-eyed, crooked-in-the-hindquarters dog named Blackie followed close behind. When we arrived in my back yard, the sloping cellar door was open. Digger looked around. "Anyone home?"

"My mom's probably in the kitchen."

"Will she see us?"

"Just be quiet," I said.

We descended into the dark, cool, familiar space, and in no time found a stack of old newspapers. I loaded Digger up until I couldn't see his eyes, then I took a pile and we staggered out unnoticed. Back at the huts, we found a stack of dead branches and rotting two-by-fours. Everyone was there, wild with anticipation.

Finally Grumble arrived with a stack of wood. He mumbled to himself as he placed the wood on the stack, then stepped back for a better look.

"It's not enough," he said. "We need more wood. And more paper." Everyone groaned.

I looked at Digger. I couldn't believe it. "Do we have to ...?"

Digger gave me an elbow in the ribs. "Let's go."

It turned out for the better. We found Blackie in the basement clawing at a stack of laundry in search of who knows what. "Get out," Digger shouted. Blackie didn't move.

I pointed upward. "Not so loud."

Digger grabbed Blackie by the collar and pulled him out the cellar door.

We really loaded up this time and could scarcely make it up the stairs. On our way back through the undergrowth, Blackie sniffed and lunged, lifting his leg for every bush.

Grumble adjusted the last few pieces of wood, then snatched the papers from Digger and me and stuffed them into the center. He stepped back and squinted.

"Yeah, that ought to do it." He motioned to us. "Stand over here. No, not there, behind me."

We pushed and elbowed for position.

He drew a match from his pocket. In the other hand he held a torch of twisted paper.

Our chant was short and totally inappropriate, yet

one we all knew: "Shit. Double shit. Triple shit and Shinola!" The tone was somber, worthy of the moment. I looked at Digger, then the others. Their eyes were glazed.

Grumble struck the match on a rock that had some ritual meaning, then lit the torch. A loud, collective "Ahh" sounded. All eyes were on the tiny flame that grew larger and larger until Grumble thrust the torch into the center of the wood.

Paper and kindling burst into flame, and soon we heard the crackling sound. I turned to the others. Faces oranged by the flames recorded a primitive joy, mouths open, eyes glistening.

I felt the sting of heat and stepped back. The flames climbed higher and higher forcing me back farther. An almost blinding brightness transformed the forest darkness. Nine filthy creatures observed, transfixed.

Then the spell was broken. A man across the alley called, "Fire!" and all hell broke loose. I screamed and ran into Digger, knocking him to the ground. Grumble hit and toppled me, and I was on my knees when Digger grabbed me. We ran across the alley into my back yard, dove down the cellar stairs into the welcome darkness, then burrowed into soiled laundry.

I turned to Digger still out of breath. "Thanks," I said.

"Shut up," he said. His jaw was tight. "We're in deep shit." It wasn't long before we heard sirens. We lay there in the dark listening to the roar of engines, men shouting, flames crackling and hissing as they were extinguished.

Finally it was more than Digger could take. "I'm going to take a look," he said.

"I'll go with you."

"You wait here." He crawled to the cellar stairs, popped his head up and looked around, then motioned for me to come up. At that moment Blackie came bounding up and licked Digger's face. "Get away, damn it," he mumbled. Blackie looked lovingly at Digger; his bad eye watered. Digger pushed him away.

Suddenly a huge, hairy arm plucked Digger off the stairs, clean and swift as a cat snapping up a mouse. Blackie barked and ran in circles, and Digger squealed like a wounded animal. I knew it was only a matter of time, but I didn't have long to suffer. A giant, blond fireman came down the stairs and hauled me out into noonday brightness.

My eyes adjusted quickly, and I looked across the smoking remains of the vacant lot. The weeds, vines, and bushes were gone. And there was no hint of where the huts used to be. Only a few large trees remained. The leaves were wilted and brown from the heat. And the smell of fire hung like a cloud.

Digger started crying and so did I. It was more than the two firemen could stand. The big blond knelt down and tried to convince us we weren't going to be harmed, then two more hauled Grumble in.

Grumble turned out to be the real actor, insisting

he didn't know a thing. I stopped crying so I wouldn't miss the performance. Even Digger quieted down, but he couldn't let it go at that. He pointed his green-stained finger at Grumble. "He did it!" he yelled. "He had the matches!"

Grumble's mouth fell open. "He's a liar!" He lunged at Digger.

Digger jumped behind the fireman's leg. "No, I'm not! I saw the whole thing." Then he pointed at me. "He brought the papers. Out of his own basement."

"What do you mean?" I shouted. "You helped me." I was appalled. Everyone was ratting.

Kids from the park had already gathered, along with a few worried mothers. I wondered why my mother wasn't there, then remembered she'd taken my sister to her piano lesson. The Turk was there—our mysterious neighbor—holding one of his cats. The driver of the black Packard was also there for a moment. He lived in a corner house with five or six other men who everyone knew were part of the mob from Chicago.

The firemen took advantage of the gathering and lectured us on the dangers of matches. I noticed Rudy standing on the front row in an older brother's stained shirt. She wore it like a dress, but she looked more like a boy with his shirt tail out. Her face was filthy, her knees scabby. She scratched a hip while another finger was thrust high into one nostril. It was apparent she was enjoying herself. I knew I was going to like her.

When the lecture was over, Digger and I were sent

home with the promise "never to play with matches."
Grumble was kept behind for more indoctrination.

On the way home Rudy tagged along. Digger nodded. "Hi, Rudy."

"Hi," she said.

"How come you weren't around this morning?"

"I had to stay home because I was in trouble." Her lisp was pronounced. Little bits of saliva flew as she spoke.

"Too bad," Digger said.

"Yeah," she said.

"This is Bradshaw," Digger said.

"Wart," I said.

"Hi." Rudy's grin showed teeth missing. "Looks like you're in twouble."

"Naw," Digger said. "We'll be all right."

I realized then that life beyond the back yard was frightening, confusing, unpredictable. I knew I never wanted to go back.

T   W   O

Digger and Rudy were my friends. I learned more
from them than I ever learned in school. They came
along at precisely the right time. It was the summer
my new life began. It stands out vividly, separated
from everything else, like oil in water. I can still see it.
Taste it. Smell it as if it were yesterday. Suddenly I
was thrust into this amazing society of kids. Of course,
there were parents, and school, and church, but life in
the group had the real impact. We were hunters, collec-
tors, builders, with an economy based on the exchange
of marbles, and a culture rich in ritual and myth.

The year was 1936. The place, northern Indiana.
And I was seven years old. The summer before was the
back yard, the sand box, my sister Mary Lou, the dull-
witted five-year-old from across the street, my mother,
safety. Digger and Rudy helped me escape.

Digger was short, square, Polish, and a year older.
His polo shirt held spots of jam on the shelf of a pot-
belly that buried his belt buckle. It was part of the
image. Primitive. Tough. Unwashed. I was never sure
how well the image worked, but I knew he attracted

flies. We all did. Bathing was not a popular or frequent event. It happened Saturday night and that was that.

Rudy was blond, Czechoslovakian, and just four months younger than I. Her real name was Ruthie, but Rudy was as close as her immigrant mother could pronounce it. And her four older brothers liked a boy's name for a little sister. She had blue eyes, rosy cheeks—the kind of face you could trust. And she was wise enough never to admit she was a girl. Otherwise Digger and I would have had nothing to do with her. It was that kind of neighborhood. Boys played with boys, and girls with girls. Rudy performed brilliantly her role as an ungendered. She used four-letter words. Sweated as much. Even spat as often. No one ever accused her of being a lady.

Digger and I learned to keep our distance when she got excited. It was her lisp. "Horse shit," her favorite expression, was deadly five feet away.

I was thin, wiry, nervous, and still unsure how to apply the freedom Digger and Rudy assumed was a natural right. I was half Polish. Mormon. Not a winning combination in the neighborhood.

Digger was older, no taller, but I could outrun him since his stomach got in the way. He had a temper. I discovered early that a swift retreat was better than wrestling. Digger kept me in line by giving me a punch, and I in turn slugged Rudy. When she complained, we reminded her that she was, after all, a "g——." But we never used the word. It was the meanest thing we could think of. It always set her straight for awhile.

We went everywhere together. To the forest preserve, marshlands, river, and open fields, hardly what one might expect less than ten miles from the steel mills and oil refineries lining the tip of Lake Michigan. Our neighborhood had large brick and stone houses with roofs of slate and tile. Spacious lawns swept down to curving streets lined with mature elms, lit at night by bronze lamps. There were a few large estates, surrounded by low stone walls, built by industrial barons during the twenties. My favorite was a sandstone manor house with a slate roof resembling a castle. Our neighbors were doctors, lawyers, scientists, industrialists who drove Buicks and Cadillacs and escaped to Europe in summer and Florida in winter. At least half belonged to the country club. The only exception was the cluster of clapboard bungalows that accounted for where Rudy, Digger, and I lived. In normal times we would have been considered the poor of the neighborhood. Because of the Depression, more than a few rich neighbors were also struggling to survive.

Each morning we met at the park that was just through the block and only several hundred feet away from the Illinois state line. Its location earned it the dubious name of Indy-Illy Park, which was an embarrassment even for seven-year-olds. We always referred to it as simply "the park." It was large enough for a tennis court, ball diamond, and a playground with swings, slide, and teeter-totter, and was always filled with kids from surrounding houses.

We'd lie on a grassy knoll under the highest tree and argue about what to do for the day. Often it took half an hour before an agreement was reached. Then we were off, free as field mice.

Of course, this is now just a memory. Digger and Rudy are lost in time, and so is Wart. We all grew up and became different people. But that hardly matters here. This is their story.

T   H   R   E   E

When I walked into the kitchen, I found my mother crying and my father trying to calm her down. He never came home for lunch. I knew I was in trouble.

My sister Mary Lou, thin, pale, never guilty of anything, sat at the table kicking the chrome leg, trying to avoid a bowl of tomato soup. My mother had a list of foods that guaranteed immunity to a host of diseases. Canned tomato soup was one of them.

My father was short, overweight, balding, and, unlike my mother, had a certain tolerance. He'd tell me stories of what he did as a boy—his way of letting me know he understood.

My mother was small, thin, and very energetic. She raced through the house cleaning, cooking, washing, arranging. Mary Lou and I were scrubbed, fed, and hovered over more than we ever wanted to be. But she never had time to read to us. There were more important things to do.

I pulled out a chair and sat down across from Mary Lou. She pushed her long curls back, then wrinkled her nose to let me know I smelled of fire. I stuck out my tongue. She returned the gesture. We got along great. I placed my elbows on the table and looked at the single wall of green cupboards. A dark oak ice box, filled twice each week with fresh ice, squatted in one corner. A sheet of patterned linoleum was worn through by the back door and under the table. A calendar, with a picture of Gibraltar from my father's insurance company, decorated the wall. There was only one window. The room was clean, dull, filled with wonderful smells.

"What's for lunch?" I said.

Everyone looked at me. Mary Lou's eyes went up. She took a spoonful of soup, swallowed, and made a face like she was taking castor oil. My father motioned for me to follow him. Mary Lou snickered. I slid off my chair and followed into the bathroom. There was no question about what was going to happen. He took down his leather razor strap, sat down on the edge of the tub, then laid the strap across his knees. He motioned for me to sit down on his lap. On the razor strap. I waited. He nodded. I sat down, and he squeezed my arm until it hurt, then held it. I turned and looked up at him. "Next time the strap," he said. "Understand?" He lifted the strap and I felt its width.

"Yes, sir," I said, then started to cry. He held me for a long time. He was warm and firm, and it felt good to be there. When I stopped crying, he kissed me and put me down. "Don't ever do that again," he said.

My father never used the razor strap. Somehow I knew he never would. Still it always got my attention.

The real punishment came from my mother. She insisted I spend the afternoon at home, which wouldn't have been bad except for Mary Lou who had to practice the piano. And the clicking sound from her tap dancing drove me crazy. My sister and I had nothing in common. We didn't even trade comic books.

The fire was bewildering. I felt guilty, realizing we had done something wrong. Yet, the excitement was enjoyable. So was the feeling of being important. Other kids in the neighborhood noticed me for the first time. And, it was really all Grumble's fault.

Life away from school was richer. The only excitement came in class from a fire drill or someone wetting their pants or throwing up. The high point of the day was draining a lukewarm bottle of milk through a straw. I didn't like school, probably because I was lousy at it.

That evening Digger and Rudy dropped by and asked if I could go out. My father was out selling insurance, so I knew there wasn't a chance. But I talked hard and finally struck a deal to be home early. I was getting on my mother's nerves.

It felt great to be free again, and right off we headed for the park. Digger didn't mention the fire, and neither did I. I was tired of the subject. But I didn't know what to think about Digger. I didn't trust him, yet I knew he could take me places and show me things I would never see otherwise. Rudy was different. I trusted her completely.

The evening was warm and sticky as honey. I stopped to tie my shoe, and succeeded after only two tries. Digger took a firefly apart, isolating the glow from the rest, and Rudy poked at a tooth she hoped was loose.

Suddenly there was shouting down the street at Grumble's house. We ran to see what was happening. The Grumbles lived in the only duplex in the neighborhood, and family fights were broadcast through the open windows on the second floor.

"If you ever do that again!" screamed Grumble's father, "you'll get a licking worse than this." Whack! Grumble was getting smacked with something flat, and he screamed every time it hit. "Here I am a fireman, and my own kid lights up the neighborhood." Whack! "Don't lie about the matches." Whack! "I know where you got them." Whack!

Digger laughed. It was wicked and uncaring. We could still hear Grumble getting it when we were a block away.

We agreed that Grumble was all right. He made mistakes. Big mistakes. And he lacked courage. And he was selfish. He was, after all, just like us.

F O U R

The vacant lot was abandoned for the rest of the summer. After the fire, like pygmies in the rain forest, we moved on. The change was no sacrifice. There was another vacant lot directly across from the park with four willow trees. We referred to all of them as "the monkey tree." They were joined together by steel cables placed there long before our time. The oldest and largest tree had a trunk eight feet around and was covered with huge knots that looked back at us like grinning ogres. Footholds were worn into the gnarled bark. Twelve feet in the air, where the trunk separated into four main branches, was an ancient tree house with a rough timber floor and only the framework of wall and roof remaining.

The cables made it possible to go from one tree to the next without touching the ground. They were about three feet apart, one for hands, one for feet—a primitive suspension bridge that took skill to negotiate, particularly at mid-span where the rusty cables sagged. You had to be tall enough to hang on to the upper cable and touch the lower one. It took practice.

There was also a single cable swing in each tree. This made it possible to swing to the ground or swing back up into another tree like Tarzan. We seldom tired of the place, even though it was dangerous. Somebody was always sporting a cast and no one ever asked how it happened. The answer was assumed. Casts, bandages, and stitches were respected symbols of courage. Every so often some parent got stirred up and tried to get the fire department to remove the cables, but they never succeeded.

The cables had been there so long they were deeply embedded in the trunks and branches. Neighborhood folklore held that a gang of ten-year-olds swiped the lumber from a construction site and built the tree house, then pulled several rolls of cable from a boxcar, and, with the help of a troop of Boy Scouts, had them out and in place before the police had time to do anything about it. The ringleader, it was said, spent time in reform school, then moved on to a life of crime.

Another myth, the one preferred by Rudy and Digger, maintained that it was built in one night by mutated beings from across the tracks. But whoever was responsible didn't matter. It was there and it was wonderful. To see the cluster of trees in silhouette at sunset, with hairless, chirping primates moving easily from tree to tree, was a spiritual experience—a direct revelation on the origin of the species. Even today, fifty years later, a visit to the zoo triggers a wrenching nostalgia.

The morning following the fire, Digger and I met at the park, then wandered over and looked at the charred remains of the lot. We could see through to the alley and the backs of houses on the other street. It was depressing. But we didn't waste time mulling over past mistakes. We walked across the street to the monkey tree and found Rudy hanging upside down from a cable. Her shirttail covered her face, and underpants, made of old flour sacks, displayed a blue and yellow Pillsbury label across her rump, an economy of the Depression.

"Hi, Digger," she lisped. Her features sagged, her eyes bulged.

"Hi," said Digger. "Want to play?"

"Sure," she said and caught Digger on the chin with saliva.

"Damn it," he said. He wiped his chin.

"Sorry," she said, and hit him again.

"Jesus, Rudy." He wiped off his arm and made a face. Rudy reached up, grabbed the cable, did a somersault and landed on her feet. A graceful move. "Sorry," she said. This time she covered her mouth.

"Just watch it." Digger could be a pain, but he was always kind to Rudy about her lisp.

"Hi Wart," she said. She raised her hand and smiled. I stared at her missing teeth until she closed her mouth.

"What shall we do?" said Digger.

"I don't know," I said, still looking at Rudy.

She shrugged.

Digger looked off. "Got an idea."

"Like what?" Rudy didn't sound convinced.

He looked hard at us. "We ought to organize a club."

"What for?" I said.

"Dumb," said Digger. "If I have to explain that." He stared off in disgust, then changed the pose. "It's like this. If you don't have a club, how can you be a member?"

"Oh," I said. I was aced. I looked at Rudy.

Her eyes narrowed. "What's it going to be about?" she lisped.

He stepped back, but too late. He wiped off his arm. "The 'I Don't Believe in Santa Claus Club,'" he said.

"What do you mean?" I said.

Rudy looked like she'd just lost a quarter.

Digger gave us an icy stare. "It's a club for guys who don't believe in Santa Claus."

"But I believe," said Rudy, almost pleading.

"You don't really, do you?" said Digger. He turned away then looked back. "You couldn't."

"What makes you so smart?" she said.

"Look. Santa Claus is fat, right?"

"Yeah," we said.

"So how can he squeeze down a damn chimney?"

"I don't know?" I said.

"And your house doesn't even have a fireplace."

That was true for the three of us.

"That doesn't matter," I said.

21

"Shit," said Digger. He turned and crawled up the trunk to the tree house. I could see him sitting there through spaces between the boards.

I turned to Rudy. "What should we do?"

"I don't know. But I'm not going to join." She looked up at Digger.

"We won't give up!" I shouted.

"We could lie," she said. Her frown relaxed into a smile that showed a cracked lip. "Yeah, let's do that."

"I'll tell him." I started up but only got half way when Digger looked over the edge.

"What do you want?" he said.

"We'll join," I said.

The corners of his mouth turned up. I motioned for Rudy to follow, and when we got to the platform Digger was sitting cross-legged like Buddha, his eyes brimming. Rudy popped through the opening in the floor, then sat down and dangled her legs over the edge. She had no fear of heights.

It was my first time. I looked down on the clutter of backyards to the park beyond and could see everything, even the house across the street that people talked about. A new, black Packard was in the driveway, and the driver was washing it. They were gangsters for sure.

"Who's going to join first?" Digger said. He brushed a crumb from his stained polo shirt.

"Do we have to decide now?" I said. "It's not even the Fourth of July."

Rudy nodded in agreement.

"Now or never," he said. "I'm the leader and I'm supposed to decide."

"Horse shit," said Rudy.

Digger dodged it.

"Who said you're the leader?" I said.

"I did. Because it couldn't be you." He chuckled. "Or Rudy." He laughed out loud and Rudy looked hurt.

"All right," I said. "But . . ."

"But what?" He stuck out his chin. "Who's going to be first?"

"Not me," said Rudy.

"Let's wait a few days," I said.

"Now," said Digger. He sat up.

"Come on, Rudy," I nodded toward the ground. "Let's talk it over."

She looked at me for a moment, then stood up, grabbed a cable, and swung easily to the ground. I wasn't sure I could do that, but I had to try. Digger's look confirmed it.

When the cable swung back up, I grabbed it and, without waiting, stepped off. Back yards and tree limbs flashed past as the ground loomed closer. I froze at the bottom and continued up. At the top of the arc I let go and dropped like wet laundry into a pile of weeds. Digger and Rudy howled with laughter. I pulled myself up and walked back to the clearing under the tree. "Come on, Rudy, let's talk."

Still snickering, she followed me behind the tree.

"Either we agree or we won't be members," I said.

Rudy thought for a moment, then nodded. We shook hands with crossed fingers.

Digger slid down the trunk and sat down in the clearing just as we came out from behind the tree. We walked around and looked down at him. "All right," I said. "We're ready. Now what?"

He played with a weed for a moment, then looked up. "We'll have to have an initiation," he said.

"What's that?" sprayed Rudy.

"It's like church," I said. "You know."

Rudy acted like she still didn't understand.

I turned to Digger. "What do you have in mind?"

"I've got a good one," he said nodding, his eyes rolled upward.

"Well?"

"Well what?" he said.

"Come on, Digger."

"The guys across the tracks tried it." He looked off absentmindedly while depetaling a dandelion. "They said it works great."

"What is it?" yelled Rudy.

"Take it easy," he said. He stood up. His eyes narrowed and he spoke slowly. Our faces were just inches apart. "It's like this. You take a lighted match, see. And after everyone repeats, 'I don't believe in Santa Claus,' you shove the lighted match into someone's wrist."

"Who's wrist?" screamed Rudy. She caught him on the forehead.

He wiped it off. "We all take a turn," he said.

"I want to be last," said Rudy before I had a chance.

Digger frowned. "There's only one fair way. We have to draw straws." He withdrew two dandelion stems.

"Wait a minute," I said. "What about you? It can't be just between Rudy and me." I knew exactly what he was doing. I'd gone through the same routine at school and lost.

It took some time to settle the drawing. I lost against Rudy first, then with Digger. He was always lucky. But there was no turning back.

Digger made me stand several feet away. He lifted a match. Scarcely a day since the fire and the guy still had matches. "Are you ready?" he said.

He lit the match.

I looked away.

"We-don't-believe-in-Santa-Claus," we chanted. I gritted my teeth and waited, but the match went out. Rudy's fault. Too much saliva from the "Santa."

"Come on, Rudy," said Digger. "Watch it."

We started again, but this time Rudy turned away as Digger lit the match. "We-don't-believe-in-Santa-Claus." Digger drove the flame into my wrist.

I screamed. Then came the pain. It was like a knife. I swung at Digger. He watched open-mouthed as my fist sunk into his cheek. I stood over him crying. He looked up, too surprised to move. I held my wrist out for everyone to see. It was red in the middle, puffed up,

25

and white around the edge. Digger began to cry.

"Who's next?" I shouted. The smell of sulfur was still in the air. I could taste it.

"Not me!" cried Rudy. She stepped back still looking at my wound.

Digger looked away.

I lunged at him. We scuffled, and somehow I retrieved a match. "All right, you guys!" I shouted. I lit the match and began the chant. "We-don't-believe . . ." It was no use. Digger and Rudy were gone.

The club was never formed. And I found there was little honor for a wounded veteran of an abandoned cause. I have the scar to this day.

F I V E

My mother put a fresh bandage on my wrist. The burn was just as painful the next day. She suggested I show Rudy and Digger I could get along without them. Besides, my sister, Mary Lou, was available. It wasn't that we did much together, but it was good therapy occasionally. It made us appreciate friends.

Adults thought Mary Lou was wonderful. She was two years older than I and did well in school. And she was pretty. But her black eyes and long curly hair exacted a terrible price. My mother, inspired by her possibilities, spent hours grooming, dressmaking, shopping, that left both exhausted and irritable. I was amazed anyone would accept that kind of punishment. It was great being plain, dull, male.

Mary Lou also took dancing and piano lessons. No lessons for me of any kind. My parents realized school was all I could manage.

Under normal conditions, Mary Lou and I could endure each other for about an hour, the exception being when we were trapped in a car and couldn't last ten minutes together. My father would stop the car, reach over in the back seat, and pull us apart. I was not looking forward to time spent with Mary Lou, merely willing to endure it.

Mary Lou sat at the table pouting, trying to decide if she could actually down the mixture of orange juice and cod liver oil our mother forced on us every morning. The trauma alone destoyed any possibility of making us healthier.

I finished breakfast and stood at the bay window in the dining room. Digger and his dog walked toward the house. A surge of anger enveloped me, but the feeling quickly passed. I was about to be entertained by the morning ritual I had noticed even before I knew Digger's name. It was always the same, and all at the expense of our neighbor, Mrs. Bean. Every kid in the neighborhood detested her. She let us know the feeling was mutual.

Mrs. Bean spent hours grooming her yard. The grass was perfect as a golf green. She was shaped like a double ice cream cone, and the flowered dress she wore every day dramatized each roll and bulge.

Mr. Bean was thin and spent all of his time indoors listening to ball games on the radio. He liked children. When he smiled and said, "Hello," Mrs. Bean muttered something and looked the other way.

Mr. Bean was also an alcoholic. We never saw him drunk, but we kept tabs on his night life. He loved his old black Oldsmobile with wooden spokes, but late at night he had difficulty getting it into the garage. He only applied the brakes after he smacked the back wall, which was slowly moving the garage into the alley. The collision would wake me and Mary Lou, and I would check it out the following morning. The garage was now a couple of feet off the foundation. My mother wondered if it would cut off access for garbage trucks, but no one dared complain. Mary Lou and I had high hopes that some night Mr. Bean would plough right through.

Digger made Mrs. Bean's lawn a prime target. I called to let Mary Lou know Digger and Blackie were coming, but she didn't answer. When Digger arrived, he gave Blackie a shove and the dog trotted out to the middle of the Beans' lawn, sniffed, and left his calling card. Digger even had time to run up and ring the doorbell.

Mrs. Bean appeared at the front door screaming and flaying the air, while Digger and Blackie turned the corner and were gone. Someday Mrs. Bean was going to catch Digger. At least that was my hope that morning.

Mary Lou skipped in. She grinned. The orange juice and cod liver oil had undoubtedly been poured down the drain when mother wasn't looking.

"Mrs. Bean got it again," I said.

"Really?" She ran to the window and looked out. "She's gone," she said. She exhaled and her shoulders dropped.

"It's your fault," I said. "But you've seen it before."

She turned from the window, smiling.

Immediately my guard was up.

"What shall we do?" she said, then cranked up her smile.

"I don't know," I said.

"Let's do something interesting," she said. Mary Lou was quick, clever, knew how to manipulate, but once she found something that worked, she repeated it too often.

"Why don't you put your hands over your head?" she said.

"Because you'll tickle me."

"I wouldn't do that."

"Yes you would."

"You have to trust me."

"Why should I?"

"Because . . . well . . . I'm your sister, that's why."

"You tickled me the last time."

"I don't remember."

Of course, it was hopeless. I stalled. She persisted. It was only a matter of time.

She had phenomenal patience. Her face must have ached from grinning. Now it was time to apply the final ploy. She turned away looking hurt. It was nauseating. But I was anxious to move on to the next step.

"All right," I said, then slowly raised my arms. She watched out of the corner of her eye until my arms were straight up. She turned, and there before me was a screaming, howling maniac, features deformed, eyes bulging. I collapsed in a desperate effort to cover myself, but she followed me to the floor, her tentacles embedded in my armpits.

I pushed. She clawed. I kicked. She punched. When I finally broke loose, I swatted her. She began to cry.

"Shut up," I said. "Mom'll hear."

"I know," she said. "You hit me." She held up her arm like she was wounded.

"What did you do to me?"

"Hardly anything," she said.

I had let it happen again. Then I remembered the time she wrenched her wrist when she wouldn't let go and she had to wear a sling for a week. A pleasant memory, but not good enough to spend more time with her.

I fixed my bandage, then walked out the back door, crossed the lawn, and headed down the alley. I knew Rudy and Digger would be at the monkey tree so I headed for the park.

On my way I passed the back fence of the mysterious Turk. Grumble was always trying to catch one of his cats. Not only was Grumble a firebug, he had a reputation for hanging cats.

I cut through the Beckers' back yard and started across the street when I noticed Bernie Heifitz on the other side. He was sitting in the shadow of an elm, nibbling on a candy bar. Even from across the street I could tell it was a Baby Ruth.

I didn't like Bernie, but that didn't matter. At least

he wasn't a friend or relative. He looked up as I approached. He was picking at the candy bar, one peanut at a time. I hoped he might offer some, but I knew he wouldn't. Rudy would have split it with me, and Digger would have given me a bite. Not Bernie. It wasn't that he needed it. He was as round as Digger, but where Digger was hard Bernie was blubber. He had red curly hair, large freckles, wore thick glasses, and was as bright as he looked.

"What are you doing?" I said.

"What does it look like?" He licked chocolate from the corner of his mouth. His tongue was brown.

"Doesn't look like you're doing anything," I said. "Just laying under a tree."

"You guessed it," he said. Chocolate drivel formed on his chin.

It was turning into a wonderful day. But then it happened. The late morning air was shattered by his mother's high-pitched, mind-bending call for lunch. It happened every day, trustworthy as the bell on the Catholic church. She drove the neighborhood crazy, particularly the dogs.

Bernie grunted as he stood up, then waddled off without saying another word. I felt lonely. This wasn't what I had had in mind. The boycott against Digger and Rudy wasn't working.

S I X

After lunch I went in search of Digger and Rudy. They weren't at the park or the monkey tree, so I tried Digger's house. His grandfather sat on the back porch cleaning his pipe. He was a small man with gray, thinning hair, and he wore bib overalls and heavy work shoes. He was pleasant, but there was a sadness about him.

"Digger around?" I said.

He rubbed his nose. "Nope. Off somewhere with his dog."

"Was he with Rudy?"

He drew on his pipe. "I think so."

I studied his pipe, wondering why people would smoke. He drew a pinch of tobacco from a leather pouch, stuffed it into the pipe, lit it, and took a deep draw. "What's that button on your shirt?"

"It says VOTE FOR LANDON," I said.

"Why would anyone vote for Landon?"

"Because he's a Republican," I said.

"I know that. And you can wear that anywhere but around here. Please take it off."

"Yes sir," I said. I could tell he was upset.

He rubbed the dust off his shoes. I knew he had been out of work for several years. I removed the pin from my shirt and stuffed it in my pocket. I walked away wondering. Even my uncle Jim, a fireman and a Catholic, was a Republican. It was confusing.

A lot of things were hard to understand. Why were there Catholics and Jews? And why was I a Mormon? The answer was simple. My father left Utah after the war in 1919, figuring there was more of a future in the Midwest. He attended the University of Chicago where he met my mother, a Polish-Catholic. They had little in common, but she was pretty and she taught him enough Polish to help him sell insurance to recent immigrants. His clients laughed at his Polish, and he laughed with them. He did pretty well.

My grandparents, who spoke no English, were stunned when my mother married a Mormon. It wasn't just leaving the Catholic church that bothered my grandfather, it was losing her heritage. But he couldn't help liking my father.

I think my mother married him because he didn't drink. My grandfather spent a lot of time at the corner saloon.

I liked visiting my grandparents. Their small house was dark inside and filled with the smell of coffee and baked bread. The furniture was a strange assortment that Mother said was bought because the price was right. The only thing on the wall was a parish calendar with a picture of Jesus with a golden halo. A large, second-hand radio, with lit-up dials that formed eyes, nose, and mouth, looked like a giant head emerging from the floor. Grandmother was sure the radio would teach her to speak English, but it never did.

My grandfather had curly gray hair and a handlebar mustache. Sometimes he wore knickers and a loden jacket with deer antler buttons. I thought he looked dashing. But he was stern. I was never sure how he felt about me.

Grandmother was easier. She was short, plump, and always wore a fresh, white apron that smelled like clean sheets. I spoke no Polish, but we got along famously playing tag, chasing each other through the house. She was over seventy but quick. I had to work hard to catch her. I knew that she liked me.

Occasionally we attended the parish church for a cousin's wedding or a relative's funeral. Mary Lou and I were supposed to follow along during the Mass—my father insisted—but we were often left standing when everyone else was kneeling. Then we'd snicker, and Mother would give us a dirty look.

I preferred Mass over the Mormon sacrament service. Mass was shorter. And there was all this standing and kneeling, and stained glass windows, alters, and statues to look at. But I was appalled by the crucifix. Jesus had haunting eyes that looked off, upward, and he had spikes in his wounds dripping blood. Why would people want a thing like that in their church? My mother's explanations didn't help. Mother didn't fit the tight Polish community. She liked the people but she preferred luncheons, teas, and bridge club. She did all her shopping at Marshall Fields, even though we could scarcely afford it. We had the best pediatrician in town, the most expensive dentist, and my sister took piano lessons from Mrs. Schwarzkopf who was almost as fat and mean as Mrs. Bean. And her German accent was hard to understand. If we weren't as rich as some of our neighbors, we were respectable. That was the important thing. Sometimes it got on your nerves.

When I finally found Digger and Rudy, they were at the monkey tree, on the platform munching apricots. After a morning with Mary Lou and Bernie, they looked good. Like finding a lost toy. The anger from the day before was gone.

"Come on up," shouted Digger. I raced to the trunk and scrambled up, proud of the way I could use the cables. I pulled myself through the platform opening.

Rudy winced when she saw the bandage on my arm. "Hi," she said. I knew she was glad to see me. She chewed with her mouth open and her chin was covered with apricot juice.

Digger took a bite, spit it out, and threw the remaining apricot over his shoulder. He handed me one, then tried another. "Saw you nailed Mrs. Bean this morning," I said.

"Blackie never fails," he said.

"Where'd you get the apricots?"

He spit out another chunk, then threw the rest away. "Old lady Becker gave 'em to us."

"They're lousy," said Rudy. Small bits of apricot arched through the air and landed on Digger.

"Jesus, Rudy." Digger wiped off his leg, then moved back a couple of feet.

Just then a black Packard pulled into the driveway across the street. The driver got out and opened the garage door. When the car was inside, four men got out, dressed in black suits, then the driver pulled the garage door down. We waited to see if anyone came out. No one. My father said there was an underground passage between the house to the garage that was built during Prohibition. Maxie Grimm, a guy in my class, had one in the house he just moved in.

"Anyway," said Digger. "The old bag figures if she gives us the crummy ones on the ground we won't climb her tree." He grinned. "Guess we'll have to wait until dark."

I took a bite. It was bitter. And there was a worm-hole. I spat it out and threw the rest away. "Maybe we should give them to Bernie?"

"I'm tired of him tagging along," Digger said. "Then getting caught."

"And he squeals on everyone else," said Rudy, this time covering her mouth.

"We'll tell him the apricots are bad this year," said Digger.

Rudy crawled over to the platform opening, avoiding rusty nails and splinters, and looked down. "Who's that?" she said. Digger and I joined her.

At the base of the tree was a boy my age in a clean white polo shirt. He pretended not to see us.

"Must be somebody's cousin," said Digger.

"Whose?" I said.

"Let's find out."

I took the cable, Digger slid down the back of the trunk, and Rudy used the foot-holes. We arrived on the ground about the same time.

The boy acted surprised but he didn't move. Digger stopped in front of him for a moment, then walked around and looked him over. The boy followed him with his eyes. Finally Digger faced him, and Rudy moved in to back him up. The boy broke a twig in half, quarters, then threw the twigs over his shoulder.

"What's your name?" said Digger.

"What's yours?" said the boy.

Digger stepped closer. "I asked first."

The boy stepped back. "Clancy," he said. "Todd Clancy."

Digger motioned for me to ask the next question. I couldn't think of anything. Digger turned to Rudy. She shrugged. There was nothing else to do. Digger gave Clancy a soft punch on the arm. Clancy punched him back. I looked at Rudy. This had never happened before. Suddenly Blackie appeared, snarling, and Rudy grabbed his collar, then realized he had just spotted a cat and let him go.

Digger punched Clancy again, this time a little harder. Clancy let him have it with a right hook. Digger grabbed his jaw, wide-eyed, speechless. Then Digger lunged. He got Clancy by the neck and tried to drag him to the ground, but Clancy twisted, spun loose, and Digger hit the ground with a thud. It knocked the air out of him; his face turned blue. Clancy jumped on, rolled him over, and sat on his chest. Digger was pinned. Rudy and I couldn't believe it.

"You didn't tell me your name," said Clancy.

"Get off my chest," gasped Digger still fighting for air.

Clancy thought for a moment, then looked up at Rudy and me. "Okay." He stood and watched Digger drag himself to his feet and brush off the weeds and dust. It was a poor attempt to let Clancy know he was lucky this time, but nobody bought it.

"Jerry Stranski," he said. He tucked in his shirt and thrust out his chest. "Everyone calls me Digger."

"What was that?" said Clancy. Digger repeated his name. Rudy and I were awed. We could never talk to Digger that way.

Blackie came back and this time he snarled at Clancy, who knelt down and patted him on the head while Blackie licked his hand. What can you say about a dog like that?

"Where do you live?" I said.

Clancy pointed to a large two-story brick house

with a broad front porch. "Over there," he said. Then I noticed the moving van in the driveway.

"Where did you come from?" said Rudy.

"From the other side of the tracks," he said. He wrinkled his nose and his eyes angled off.

"Wait a minute." Rudy pointed. "Over there?"

"Yeah."

She looked at me not believing. Clancy looked just like us. None of the mutations Grumble warned us about. More proof that Grumble was not to be trusted.

"I didn't want to move," said Clancy. "We had lots of neat places to go."

"Bet we have more," said Digger.

"What grade are you in?" I said. The sound of the word "grade" was depressing.

"Second grade," he said.

"Me, too," said Rudy.

"Third," said Digger.

I didn't answer.

"What grade are you in?" said Clancy.

"Oh, second," I said.

Clancy looked at me. "Why didn't you say so?"

"He doesn't like school," said Digger.

"I hate it," I said.

Clancy studied me for a moment, then shrugged. "I'd like to try the tree," he said.

I motioned for him to follow. Digger and I raced up the trunk, and from the tree house platform we sailed across the double cables to the second tree, then took the swing cable to the third. We looked back and saw that Clancy had barely arrived at the platform. Finally, he took the first cable.

"Kind of clumsy," said Digger.

"Give him a chance," I said.

In less than an hour Clancy could do everything, hang upside down, swing high and out, and scramble across the cables. He was good all right. But he would never equal Rudy. None of us could. We figured it was the strength in her shoulders. Some days she was spectacular.

When we returned to the platform, Clancy turned to Rudy. "You're pretty good," he said.

"You're not bad yourself," she said. Suddenly I was jealous.

S E V E N

Rudy and I were lying on our backs, enjoying the smell of freshly mowed grass and studying the animal shapes in the clouds. Clancy was home in bed with the three-day measles he got the day after he moved into the neighborhood. And Digger was late returning from lunch. It was Thursday, still two days away from our Saturday night bath, and we were swatting flies. Rudy nudged me, and I looked up as Digger came strolling up.

"Guess what?" said Digger. He looked down and talked out of the corner of his mouth like he always did when he was selling or lying. "I've got it all lined up." He stood there stiff-legged, his chin out, his nostrils flared. A large fly buzzing around his head disturbed the pose. Finally, he spun around and took a swing at it.

"What lined up?" I said, trying to sound bored.

"Diane Dunster," he said. His eyes grew large.

"For what?" said Rudy.

I stopped picking the scab on my knee.

His eyes narrowed. "She wants to know what boys

look like." He paused. "And I want to know what girls look like."

I turned to Rudy. She shrugged. "What do you mean?" I chuckled and tried to act dumb.

"You know," he said, then pointed.

"Oh that," she said. "Don't you know?"

Digger was obsessed with where babies came from. Some days that's all he talked about. But Rudy tended to drift off and not pay attention.

"Nope," he said. He pursed his lips and shook his head.

"I thought everybody knew," she said.

"Well, I don't," said Digger. He kicked at some grass clippings. Finally, a broad grin replaced the frown. "You can join us," he said. "Both of you."

"You mean trade a look?" Rudy said.

"Yep."

I turned to Rudy. Her face looked drawn, pale. "Not me," she said, then slowly stood up.

"Me neither," I said.

"What's wrong with you guys?" His face wrinkled up like a red pepper. I tried to think of something.

"Because we already know," she said.

"All right. I'll do it without you." He took a full swinging kick at some grass clippings, then walked off.

Rudy wrinkled her nose. We laid back down and returned to the clouds.

Digger's curiosity about reproduction was insatiable. He always had a new theory on how the baby got into the mother's stomach. How the baby got out never progressed beyond the digestive system. Rudy told him he didn't know what he was talking about, but he just rattled on. We'd complain, but nothing stopped him. Rudy and I hoped it might go away.

Dunster was all Digger could talk about that evening. And Rudy and I were dragged into the deal, as judges. Digger never liked simple ceremonies. He normally insisted on using fire and water, but, as hard as he tried, he couldn't think of an application. He had agreed to a time and place and didn't want to mess up a meeting he was convinced would change his life.

After lunch the following day, Rudy and I headed for the equipment shed, an old wooden building in the center of the park. It was in a dense cluster of trees, ideal for the meeting with Dunster. Digger informed us that morning of what our role was to be. He and Dunster had resolved everything.

We found Digger walking back and forth through the trees, his eyes wild. He wasn't talking. We sat down and waited. Digger continued pacing. When Rudy mentioned that Dunster was late, I thought Digger was going to smack her.

I suggested that maybe Dunster was sick or something, but Digger refused to discuss it. At least he agreed to sit down. Marbles rattling in his pocket drove me crazy. Finally Rudy and I walked off leaving him slumped against the equipment shed.

We went to the apple orchard behind Becker's

house to see how the fall crop was coming, then dropped by Clancy's house and threw stones at his window. When his spotted face appeared, we were shocked. He looked like he'd been attacked by a swarm of bees. Rudy burst out laughing. We waved and walked on. It must have made Clancy feel great. We returned an hour later. Digger was still sitting there.

"Come on," I said. "Let's do something. She's not coming." The words sounded cruel.

"She'll be here," he said.

"Not a chance," said Rudy. But she was wrong. I could see Dunster crossing the street less than a block away.

"Here she comes," I whispered, like I was stalking a butterfly.

Digger jumped up. "Where?" His eyes were on fire.

I pointed.

"Dammit," said Rudy. "I thought we . . ."

"Shut up," said Digger. His eyes narrowed as he wet his lips.

"Maybe you could do it tomorrow after lunch?" said Rudy.

Digger spun around and smacked her on the arm, which didn't follow protocol.

Dunster walked past us without saying a thing, then stopped, looked both ways, and darted into the trees. Digger nodded for us to follow. It took time for my eyes to adjust to the dim light. The air was stick-hot, the undergrowth smelled like rotten leaves. Birds chattered, crickets chirped, leaves whispered. Dunster plucked leaves from a bush. She was tall, thin, pale, wore glasses—a year older than Digger.

"Where you been?" said Digger.

"Tap-dancing lesson," said Dunster.

"Horse shit," said Rudy.

Dunster glared at her.

Digger stepped between them. "Shut up," he said. Rudy and Dunster continued eye contact.

Finally, Digger nodded and we took our places. Dunster and Digger faced each other about five feet apart, and Rudy and I stood the same distance behind Dunster. Digger explained the procedure one more time.

"And whoever loses the toss has to go first, right?"

"Yeah," said Dunster still looking at the ground. The difference between the two was amazing. Digger was ecstatic. Dunster looked depressed. I couldn't figure out why she had agreed to do it.

"It has to last for ten counts," he said.

"Five," she said. "We already agreed." She pressed her lips together until they disappeared.

"All right, five," he said. He reached into his pocket, and his face showed panic. I could hear the marbles. When he finally withdrew a penny, he looked relieved.

"Heads," she said, as the penny flew up, then landed at her feet. She bent down for a closer look. Digger dropped to his knees.

"Tails," he said. He looked up, the corners of his

mouth turned up.

"Two out of three," said Dunster. She pushed her hair back and adjusted her glasses. Her upper lip was sweating.

"What do you mean?" he said.

"It's always two out of three," snapped Dunster.

Digger snatched the coin and stood up.

Dunster won the next two tosses, then Digger insisted on three out of five. Digger won that round, and it was finally decided at six out of ten with Dunster still the loser.

"Can we get this over with?" I said.

There was grumbling all around as we took our places. The air was charged, and I felt confused, uncomfortable. My skin was hot, tingling.

Dunster was shaking, yet her jaw was set. She wrinkled her nose and her glasses jumped up and down. I felt sorry for her. She dropped her underpants around her ankles, with her skirt still down, then stood there, knees locked. My assignment was to make sure everything was fair, and Rudy was supposed to do the counting. It was a mistake. Rudy wasn't good under pressure.

I shouted, "Up!" Rudy started counting. "One, two..." Dunster lifted her skirt, then looked away gritting her teeth. Digger stared.

He really got his money's worth because Rudy couldn't remember what followed four. She knew, but she'd buckled under before. Dunster dropped her dress before the count of five.

Digger's face looked black. "Wasn't anything there," he said. "Just like a statue." His shoulders slumped.

"What do you mean?" shouted Dunster.

"Sure you were looking at the right place?" I said.

Digger didn't answer. I thought he was going to cry.

"What did you expect?" I said.

"I don't know. I just don't know." His voice faded off.

"Okay," said Dunster. "Your turn." Her eyes loomed large behind her glasses.

Digger came out of his stupor. "I didn't get a full five counts," he said.

"What do you mean?" screamed Dunster. She lunged at him, but the underpants at her ankles tripped her. She landed on her face.

Digger looked down at her. "A full five counts," he said. He held up five fingers.

"No way!" she screamed. She squirmed as she pulled up her drawers, then lunged again. She caught his ankle, and he toppled like a tin soldier.

It took ten minutes to pull them apart. Then we had to calm them down. Digger was stubborn. "A full five counts," he said. Rudy had to hold Dunster back.

Digger folded his arms. "Okay Dunster, five more, and I'll do it for ten." He waited. I couldn't believe him.

"All right," she said. "Five counts for ten." She pushed Rudy aside and pointed at me. "You count this time. If you can?" I quickly proved myself by counting to five.

"All right," she said.

Digger took his position and she dropped her drawers. I shouted, "Up!" Dunster's skirt went up. Digger stared. "One, two, three, four, five." Dunster's skirt came down.

Silence descended like dropped sand. I watched Digger's face work through a terrible confusion. He looked at the ground then returned to me. He tried to form words, but nothing came. He snapped his head back and turned to Rudy. "Is that all there is?"

Rudy stared back in anger, the color drained from her face. She nodded yes.

At first I wondered why he would ask Rudy, then I remembered. And for a long moment we stood glaring at each other, immobilized by the chasm that separated gender. Then came the leap to the defense of one's own kind. Rudy's eyes let me know that she had fled to the other side. Her side.

Then all hell broke loose. Dunster's face turned red and Digger screamed. "No deal! It's all off! I mean that's like trading a steely for a glassy."

Dunster's eyes were giant discs.

"You know Digger!" I shouted. "You're not exactly . . ."

Dunster swung at Digger, missed, and hit me in the arm. I smacked her back. She hit me and raised a hickey. By then, Digger was gone. He looked like a small, fast-moving dog halfway across the park. Dunster had long legs and was fast, but she didn't have a chance. I was shocked when Dunster used every cuss word I'd ever heard.

Digger didn't show up at the park that evening. Rudy and I waited until it was almost dark, then walked past his house. Blackie, looking his ugly, one-eyed best, was lounging on the back porch snapping at flies. No lights were on. We decided not to knock.

The following morning, Digger didn't show up at the park. Rudy and I stuck around until we got so bored we had to do something. All we accomplished was a trip to the fields where we swiped some carrots, then went home to lunch. That's where I found out what had happened.

Mary Lou was a friend of Dunster and said it was all over the neighborhood. Dunster told her how she waited outside Digger's house the night before, and when he came out she let him have it with fists and feet and everything else. But that was nothing compared to the following morning when she waited for him in a tree. Mary Lou saw the whole thing.

"Dunster dropped on him," she said. "Like a cat with its claws out. He froze and screamed like he'd already been hit. She clawed him up pretty bad, then whipped him with a leather belt. She's got a temper."

It must have been terrible. When Digger came to the park that afternoon, his body was orange with Merthiolate. When Rudy complained he was too bright a color to go swiping tomatoes, he broke down and cried.

Dunster nailed him that night on the way home, and again the following morning. The guy could hardly turn around. It got to be ridiculous. Finally Digger's granddad had a talk with Dunster's father, which reduced the frequency but not the intensity of the attacks.

Digger was never the same. Wherever he went, he looked over his shoulder or up into the trees. The slightest sound made him jump. When he arrived at the park with a black eye, or a new bandage, we never asked him to explain. He was a fugitive in his own neighborhood. He never found peace until Dunster moved away. He paid a terrible price.

Once he even offered Dunster ten counts when she was whacking him with a snow shovel. She said she wasn't interested. We found out later that Grumble provided the service for a nickel a second. Mary Lou said that amounted to fifty cents. Ten Baby Ruth bars. Digger was sick when he heard about it.

E I G H T

The afternoon Clancy came back, we spent several hours in the trees. It turned into a wild game of tag. We climbed, crossed over, swung, occasionally fell, but no one got hurt. Finally we gathered in the cool shade of the tree house and looked down on Blackie who was attempting but failing to catch a grasshopper.

"What's next?" said Rudy.

"I don't know," said Digger.

"How about Rudy's house?" I said.

"Yeah." Rudy grinned at Clancy.

"Good idea," said Digger, then smacked the tree trunk with the underside of his fist.

"What's this all about?" said Clancy.

"You'll see," I said.

We flew out of the tree, each one taking a different way to the ground, then raced through the gray vacant lot where dry ashes blew in a soft breeze. Down the alley, through my yard, along Locust Street past the Turk's house, we stopped in front of a dull, white bungalow.

No one explained to Clancy that Rudy's house was

famous for its clothes chute. Even my sister was aware of it, and she didn't know much of anything important. Rudy bragged about seeing kids she didn't even know lined up in the hall, waiting their turn. It was that spectacular. But the traffic drove her mother nuts. We followed Rudy round to the back door and entered. The house was much like ours—living room, dining room, and kitchen on one side, two bedrooms and a bath on the other. The kitchen was large. A huge beat-up table sat in the middle of the floor surrounded by a variety of chairs painted different colors. There was no linoleum, only an oak floor with all the varnish worn off. The calendar on the wall had a frightening picture of Jesus. A crown of thorns covered his head. And a white crucifix hung over the wooden ice box. The place smelled of beer.

We passed into the dining room, empty except for a rag rug that looked lost in the middle of the floor. Rudy's mother came roaring out of the living room. Everyone froze. She was a giant. She could have passed for Mrs. Bean's sister except that she wasn't fat, and her skin looked red and blotchy. She shouted something at Rudy the rest of us couldn't understand.

"What did she say?" said Clancy.

"I can't say it in English," said Rudy.

"Yes, you can," said Digger. "Just think about it."

"If the little bastards make mess I kill you!" shouted her mother. She had false teeth but wasn't wearing them. "That's English, no?" She stood there

53

glaring at us, hands on hips, feet spread apart. No one spoke. She wasn't wearing shoes, and I studied her feet. She had hammer toes, corns, bunions, and whatever else could go wrong with the human foot. They were the ugliest living forms I had ever seen. Finally she rushed past us into the kitchen. Digger snickered.

"I'm sorry," Rudy said. She looked embarrassed.

Clancy shrugged it off, but I could tell he was shocked. So was I.

"Come on," said Rudy. We followed her into the hall. I suddenly heard Rudy's voice, as if it were coming out of a deep well. "Who's next?" she yelled. The sound echoed upward. Then I saw the opening. It was large enough to walk into standing up.

Digger gave a Tarzan shriek then dropped into the hole. Clancy looked nervously at me. I stepped off into darkness and dropped into a mound of laundry. My heart was pounding. Digger pulled me off in time to avoid Clancy following right behind.

"Great!" shouted Clancy.

"Want to go again?" said Rudy.

"Sure." Clancy rolled to his feet. "We had one just about as good in the other neighborhood."

"But not as big," I said.

"Not quite," said Clancy.

We passed the coal furnace squatting like an octopus with ducts fanning out across the ceiling. A loud voice stopped us. "Where are you going?" We turned. There was Rudy's father, clippers in hand, giving her oldest brother a haircut. Three other brothers were lined up according to age, waiting their turn. Sunlight from a basement window cast a patch of light across the basement floor.

"Get in line," mumbled her father.

"Not now," she said.

"Now!" he yelled, then nodded toward the rear of the line. Rudy's brothers, all blonds, looked like the same boy at different ages. Rudy looked just like them, and her haircut wasn't that different. Her youngest brother Mike motioned for her to line up.

"Horse shit," said Rudy. I waited for a scolding, but her father said nothing.

Rudy's father was handsome, wore a mustache, and was much shorter than her mother. He was a fireman. On paydays when he wasn't on duty, he went to the bar, then came home all fired up to cut hair. His way of celebrating. Rudy said he'd always wanted to be a barber. It was clearly the wrong day to show off the clothes chute.

Rudy stomped over and took her place in line, then turned and kicked the white-washed basement wall. She left a black mark. Mike, two years older, spun around and whacked her on the side of the head. Her face wrinkled up, but she didn't cry. Instead she gave him a haymaker to the flat of his back that sent him sprawling into the next brother. They fell forward like dominoes, the final one ending up in the lap of the brother in the chair.

"All right!" shouted her father. "Stop it!" He staggered back and looked down the line trying to focus. "Who did it?"

"He started it!" screamed Rudy. She pointed at Mike.

"I did not!" shouted Mike.

"All right, quiet!" Her father stood there weaving back and forth. "That's better," he mumbled, then belched crisp as a gun shot. He smiled, steadying himself with the back of the chair.

"How long is this going to take?" said Digger.

"Not long," said Rudy. She sighed.

The oldest boy stood, removed the sheet, shook off the loose hairs, then walked over to a discolored mirror that hung from a rough wood column. He studied himself for a moment, then walked off while the next brother took his place in the chair.

The haircut was efficient. No sideburns. Everything shaved clean to the top of the ear, all the way around. The remainder was parted in the middle. The Chico Marx look.

In no time the second brother was finished, but I noticed the shaved area had crept up higher.

"Want to try it?" said Rudy. She snickered.

Digger looked at me. "Why not?" he said. Then he looked at Clancy.

"I'm game," said Clancy.

I didn't have a choice.

Rudy didn't give us time to change our minds. "Get

in line," she said. "He won't notice the difference."

Digger laughed as he pushed me in line first. I grabbed Clancy and pulled him in front of me. I didn't trust Digger and wanted to make sure we were ahead of him. I looked up at the cobwebs and spiders on the ceiling joists. I was interested in the underside of things.

Clancy was seated after Mike was finished. No hesitation on anyone's part. The fact his hair was brown made no difference to the barber. Clancy chuckled when his head was shaved around the ears. So did I. Then it was Digger's turn. The barber stopped for only a second to peer around at Digger's face covered with Merthiolate. Then he shrugged it off. He was very drunk.

We all got a haircut except for Rudy. She was clever. Outside in the sunlight, we could see the full impact. I pointed and howled at Clancy. He let go with a punch on the arm and mussed up what was left of my hair. Digger just danced around. We had a great time pushing and shoving and bragging about all the money we'd saved. Official haircuts cost a quarter and they were painful. The barber's clippers pulled as they cut. Rudy's dad used a straight razor that cut clean and painless. As drunk as he was, his hand was steady. Or maybe we were lucky.

On our way home, we sensed a new bond, a brotherhood. But at home we caught hell. Clancy said his mother cried, and Digger got a licking from his grandfather. Mother was shocked when I first walked in, but Mary Lou burst out laughing, then my father joined in, and pretty soon we were all laughing. Mother made me look in the mirror and decide how I was going to part it. It was pretty bad.

"What do you think?" said my father. "Should I get the scissors and trim him up?"

"You'd make it worse," she said.

"Did Rudy get hers cut?" said Mary Lou.

"No," I said. "But she wanted to. Now she doesn't look like us."

"Who'd want to?" said Mary Lou. I punched her on the arm.

"Enough," said my father.

My mother frowned. "Sometimes I wonder about that girl's family. The father drinking and all."

"They drink beer," I said. "Rudy has a glass for dinner."

"You're not serious."

"A small glass," I said. I showed two inches with finger and thumb.

"For heaven's sake. Aren't you glad we don't live like that?"

"Yes," I said, but it was a lie. A glass of beer would have beat orange juice and cod liver oil any day.

N I N E

Digger was pushing to visit the pickle factory and forest preserve. It was the day after the haircuts, and we were lying on our backs at the park, listening to a noisy robin. Both places were across the state line. Forbidden by parents. All the more intriguing.

"Who likes the pickle factory?" said Rudy.

"You do," said Digger. He rolled over and faked a punch. Rudy pulled away.

"It's boring," she said. The truth was the place scared her silly. Digger told me. He and Rudy had gone with Grumble and her brother Mike, and Rudy refused to go in. I had never been there, but I saw the building every Sunday on the way to church. It was a large, sagging wreck of a barn. An old sign painted on the wall that faced the road was weather beaten, impossible to read. The building hadn't been used for years, but huge vats were still filled with a fermented brine. Boards were missing in the walls and roof, but it was still dark inside, perfect for the giant rats that darted in and out. It was a nightmare. We loathed it. It drew us like a magnet.

There were horror stories of people who had fallen into the vats and been devoured, bones and all. Grumble said a whole Boy Scout troop disappeared that way. It made you wonder how cucumbers ever made it through.

We told Clancy about it on the way, while Rudy stayed a few feet behind to be spared the details. Clancy shrugged it off, but when he caught sight of the barn, he started to sweat.

"What do you think?" said Digger.

"What am I supposed to think?" said Clancy. He thrust out his chest, but his voice cracked. No one spoke until we reached the shadow of the barn's sagging walls.

"Should I go first?" said Digger. He was grinning. No one answered. "Come on you guys."

"Yeah," said Clancy. I nodded, still thinking about flesh-eating brine. It was like seeing a movie about a crocodile then going swimming in a swamp.

I looked at Rudy. "You coming?" Digger slid back a loose plank and stepped inside.

"No, thanks," she lisped. "I've been through too many times." Her smile was transparent.

"Suit yourself," I said. I turned and followed Clancy into the fetid blackness.

"Watch it," whispered Clancy when I bumped into him. We waited for our eyes to adjust.

"What was that?" said Clancy.

I saw Digger brush his foot across Clancy's ankle.

"Probably a rat," said Digger. "Try not to step on any."

Clancy didn't answer.

I could see the first vat, big as a school bus. Digger had explained the procedure. All three vats had to be crossed to make it an official visit.

He moved out. I could barely see him in the dim light. He must have got himself stirred up about the rats because he lifted each foot high. We followed to the heavy timber ladder that led to the top of the vat. Digger crawled up, and I could hear the squeak of the plank as he walked across. I followed Clancy up the ladder. At the top, he froze. I could see the plank and the black brine about two feet below. When Clancy started across, his knees shook, rattling the plank, but he made it. I followed, looking only at the top of the plank, then crawled down the ladder on the other side. It felt wonderful to touch the ground.

We followed Digger to the second vat. It was larger, but the plank was heavier and didn't sag as much in the middle. We were across and down in no time, then proceeded to the third vat. Digger was now well ahead. And I could barely see Clancy. I climbed the ladder and realized this was the largest vat. Worse, the brine was only inches below and the plank was soaked. Probably Digger's fault. I suddenly felt alone in this vast, stinking darkness. I started across, dropped to my knees and crawled, sloshing in an inch of brine that covered the plank at mid-span. My hands and knees were wet.

I was frantic.

I practically fell down the ladder, then ran toward Digger and Clancy waiting by a long slit of light.

"Jesus, you smell awful," said Digger.

"I know," I said. "What's going to happen to my knees?"

"Better get it washed off," said Clancy. We stepped out into sunlight, sucking air.

"What took you so long?" said Rudy as she walked out from behind a bush pulling up her drawers.

"What do you mean?" said Digger. "That was fast."

"And it was pretty good," said Clancy. He was grinning.

"Just pretty good?" I said.

"It was great," said Clancy. He sniffed and rubbed his nose. From that moment he never mentioned his old neighborhood again.

Rudy squinted into the sun. "Are we still going to the forest preserve?"

"Damn it, we didn't bring potatoes," said Digger. He smacked the side of his leg.

"What do we need potatoes for? said Clancy.

"We always bake potatoes," said Rudy. It was news to me. "I know where we can get some," she said. "The store across from your school."

The word "school" cut through me like a knife. I didn't want to think about that. Rudy went to Catholic school, so she didn't know about our prison.

"Who's got some money?" said Digger. Everyone

dug in their pockets. I had three pennies, Digger had a nickel, and Rudy a dime. Clancy had no money at all, but I was surprised that Rudy was carrying around that much money. Two Baby Ruth bars. A comic book.

"Eighteen cents all together," said Clancy.

"What do you mean?" I said.

"That's what it adds up to," said Clancy. "How many will that buy?" I could never work out a story problem that fast.

"Maybe four," said Digger. "If they're small."

We headed for the store, which was only a little out of the way. During school, we'd go there to buy lemon drops, five for a penny. The only thing that got me through long afternoons. I stored them high in my cheek like a squirrel. It made them last. Inside the gray-haired grocer looked glad to see us and asked what the smell was.

"Old pickles," said Clancy.

"Smells like it," said the grocer.

I was still worried about my knees.

Eighteen cents bought five medium-sized potatoes. The grocer put them in a sack and we strutted out like a winning team.

We arrived at a different part of the forest and it took some time before we found a path. Digger finally recognized the area and said his favorite campsite wasn't far away. The forest was cool, silent. A breeze rustled the leaves, and we could hear birds, frogs, crickets. It was darker now, the air filled with the rich smell of forest floor.

"This is great," I said, but no one paid attention. They were poking around in dead leaves trying to find a mouse, a snake, anything that moved. On a nature hike last spring, half the guys in my class caught poison ivy and had to stay home for a week. I wasn't one of the lucky ones.

We passed several campsites. "Why don't we make camp here?" said Clancy.

"Just a little farther," said Digger.

"What difference does it make?" I said.

Digger looked over his shoulder. The campsite was not negotiable. When we finally found the place, Rudy and Digger were ecstatic.

"What's the big deal?" I said.

"Looks like all the others," said Clancy.

"But this is where we came before," said Rudy.

"So?" I said.

Digger gave me a shove. "Don't be a dumb shit."

"This is fine," said Clancy.

"It's okay," I said. There wasn't much there, just two logs facing a mound of gray ashes surrounded by rocks.

"Get some firewood," said Digger. "I'll dig the pit."

"What pit?" Clancy said.

Digger shot him a dirty look.

"Never mind," I said.

Clancy and I went for firewood. And when we returned, Digger had the pit already dug. He explained that the potatoes should be covered with several inches of sand, then the fire would be built on top. We argued about who got which potato, then placed them in the pit so we could claim the right ones when they were dug up. Digger covered them with sand. Dry leaves and twigs were placed on top, then larger pieces of wood until it was all to his liking. He lit a match. We watched as the flame grew and the smell of burning wood filled the air. This was one way Digger controlled. He always had matches.

The potatoes took well over an hour, so we had time to sit back and listen to Digger's latest theory on reproduction. When that got too ridiculous, even Digger was glad to change the subject. He reported on whose tomatoes were ready to swipe and whose apples looked good for later in the season. Digger liked to control the conversation.

We played tag, then hide-and-go-seek. When Digger said the potatoes were ready, we raced back. Charred embers were all that remained. "Sometimes the potatoes don't turn out perfect," he said, squinting from the smoke. "Once they turned into cinders. And last time they were raw in the middle."

He always prepared us for the worst. His leadership depended on it. We dug up the potatoes, but they were black and too hot to touch. Rudy and Digger argued over which one was theirs. I couldn't see they were worth the fight. But once they cooled down and we removed the burned surface, they tasted pretty good.

"They're better than last time," said Digger.

"Lots better," lisped Rudy. The "lots" drove small chunks of potato across the pit at Clancy.

"For chrissake, turn your head," said Digger.

"Sorry," she said, generating another barrage. Digger shook his head.

When I finished, I leaned back on the log and looked up at the sky through leaves. A perfect day. I looked at Digger and he had that satisfied look he always had after eating.

"I think we better go," said Rudy.

"Jeez, not yet," said Clancy. He was poking at the remaining embers.

"Is it that late?" said Digger.

"I think so," said Rudy. "I don't want to be here when it turns dark." It wasn't even time for dinner, but the thought of the forest at night was something to think about.

"First we have to put out the fire," I said. I threw a handful of dirt on the embers.

"Not that way," said Clancy. He jumped up and unbuttoned his fly.

"Good idea," said Digger. He jumped up and so did I. It was automatic. The way man had extinguished fire since the beginning of time. Fire and water. The perfect ritual. Soon we were enveloped in rancid smoke. Then I realized that Rudy was gone. I looked over my shoulder and spotted her some distance away. Our eyes met. She turned and ran. I called out before I thought, then the whole, immense tragedy struck like a hammer blow. Rudy could never help put out the fire, drown a colony of ants, nail a grasshopper, or write her name in the snow.

"What's wrong with him?" said Clancy. He nodded in Rudy's direction.

"There's nothing wrong with him," I mumbled.

"What do you mean?"

"Jesus," Digger said. "Rudy's a girl."

Clancy's mouth fell open. "How was I to know?" Digger looked disgusted.

"You should have said something. I mean the way she talks." Clancy shrugged. Digger shook his head. I couldn't imagine that Clancy didn't know. Clancy was smart, but sometimes he missed the big picture.

We finished off the fire, but the joy was gone. And when we caught up with Rudy, there was nothing to say.

After that, things were never the same. Rudy said "horse shit" twice as often, and we still wrestled, and I threw her to the ground, but I was careful. I didn't like it, and I sensed she didn't either. We somehow understood that's how it had to be.

It was confusing. Why should everything depend on how you took a leak? Stupid. I wondered why it wasn't something more important.

T E N

It was morning, the Fourth of July, and Digger arrived at the park with a sack full of firecrackers. They were against the law, which made them more fun. Digger found them in the vacant lot where the fire had been.

They were large, powerful, and perfect for blowing tin cans high in the air. We wandered down one alley after another dispatching cans into back yards and on to garage roofs. We got pretty good at aiming by placing the firecracker in the right spot. It was inevitable that Mrs. Bean's rose bushes became a prime target. We were in the alley behind Clancy's house. On the second try, Mrs. Bean came screaming out her back door. Too late. The firecracker exploded and the can went haywire, sailing through the window of Clancy's garage. The sound of glass breaking stopped Mrs. Bean for a moment. We took off. She chased us, but only a short distance. It was all she could manage. Clancy said his dad would raise hell if he found out about the window.

Mrs. Bean went back in the house, and we noticed the Beans' garage had moved even further into the alley. We thought that was hilarious. Then Clancy got an idea. "If we had the right stuff, we could blow the garage back into place."

"Come on," said Digger. "That'd take dynamite."

"Or thirty firecrackers," said Clancy. "All going off at the same time."

"How you going to do that?" said Digger.

Clancy bit his lip. "What if we made one big firecracker?"

"Yeah," I said. "One big one would do it." I looked around. Everyone was grinning.

"How you going to make one?" said Digger.

"We'll shake the powder out of a bunch of firecrackers," said Clancy. "Then wrap it in a newspaper."

"Will that work?" I said.

Clancy stiffened. "Why wouldn't it?"

"I wouldn't bet on it," said Digger. "And they're my firecrackers."

"Come on," I said. "Let's try."

"All right. But if it fails . . ."

"It won't," said Clancy. His eyes sparkled. "I'll be right back." He ran into his garage and returned with a newspaper. Without asking, he took a handful of firecrackers and broke them in half, allowing the powder to fall on the opened paper. When he finished the first handful, he asked for more. Digger griped about it but caved in.

"That ought to do it," said Clancy. "If it doesn't blow it back in place, it ought to move it a little."

"You sure?" said Digger.

Clancy shrugged. "What have we got to lose?"

"Bean's garage," said Rudy.

Everyone glared at her.

Clancy wrapped the paper in a roll and placed a string inside to be used as a fuse. It was impressive. He quickly placed the roll under the corner of the garage where it hung off the foundation. Digger, still in control of the matches, was right behind him.

After several attempts to light the string, Clancy grabbed a match and set the paper on fire. We ran. There was a loud hissing sound. We looked back in time to see the roll swirling around, then flames from the burning paper licked up the side of the garage. Fortunately the fire went out. We walked back to the garage and studied the large blackened area.

"Kind of a mess," said Digger.

Clancy scratched his head. "Must have done something wrong."

"I guess," said Rudy.

Clancy looked dead serious. "We should have wrapped the paper tighter. Let's try . . ."

"No," said Digger.

"I know I could make it work."

"Sure," said Digger. He walked off and Rudy and I followed. Clancy brought up the rear. I was really disappointed. I wanted Clancy to succeed, just to show Digger he was wrong. It would have changed the balance of power. Clancy didn't know everything, but moving the garage became his obsession. Every couple of days he'd mention some wild idea, but no one listened.

That was also the morning we spotted the Turk in his yard. He lived alone in the small bungalow next to the Beans and usually left early in the morning and returned late at night. My father sold him fire insurance for the pool hall he owned. He said the Turk had a good business.

Digger was interested in the grape arbor, the only one in the neighborhood. The vines looked promising. When we passed the Turk's fence on the alley, Digger dropped to his knees and looked through a knothole. "You've got to see this," he said. He was there only a second before he spun around. "The Turk's in there," he whispered.

"Who?" whispered Rudy. She was ready to run.

"The Turk. It's him." He pointed with his thumb. "Take a look."

I looked through the knothole. It was the Turk all right. He was barefoot and wore rolled-up pants and an undershirt. His back was covered with black hair, and a cigar protruded from his bushy mustache. Little puffs of smoke came out of his nostrils as he carefully watered the vines with a garden hose. He stopped for a moment and poured milk in a dish for some baby kittens, then returned to watering.

Everyone got a good look before we headed down the alley. "I don't know," said Clancy. "I'd hate to be caught swiping his grapes."

71

"Yeah," said Rudy. "He looks mean."

Digger smiled. "Let's wait and see how good the grapes are."

We didn't blow up any more cans that day. Digger thought we should save the firecrackers for something important and we all agreed except Clancy.

There was more spying to do. We checked on neighbors with gardens and fruit trees. This time we also stopped to check the Heifitz back yard. They were Jewish, and, since they didn't believe in Jesus, Clancy was certain there would be strange goings-on in their back yard. Nothing was out of the ordinary except that Bernie's mother stepped out on the back porch and called him to lunch. That took care of our curiosity.

We returned to the tree house and sat around kind of bored and irritable, going down on the last of Becker's cherry crop. Digger told Rudy she looked disgusting with a ring of cherry stain around her mouth. Just then the black Packard pulled into the driveway across the street. We watched as the driver—a short, fat man wearing a black suit—jumped out and pulled up the garage door. He drove into the garage. Two other men in black suits got out of the car and one pulled the door down.

"They must be rich," said Clancy.

"Hah," said Digger. "They're rich all right."

"Gangsters are always rich," lisped Rudy.

"My dad told me all about them," said Clancy.

"So did my granddad," said Digger. "See how they

just disappeared." We continued to watch. The garage was at least fifty feet from the house, and no one had yet emerged from the garage.

"What do you mean, disappeared?" said Clancy. He spit out a cherry stone.

"Did you see anyone come out of the garage?" said Digger.

"Nope," said Clancy.

"They don't live in the garage," said Rudy. She snickered and drooled cherry juice.

"They use the secret passage," I said. "There's a tunnel that connects the house and garage."

"Really?" said Clancy

"Yeah," I said, amazed that Digger hadn't taken over yet. He had a mouthful of stones. "They used to store whiskey in the underground passage. Then they'd take it out and sell it. It was against the law."

Digger spit out the stones. "It wasn't against the law."

"Yes, it was. My dad said so."

"That isn't what my granddad said."

"Never mind," said Clancy. "I'll ask my father. He's a lawyer." He said "lawyer" as if that meant some kind of magic. It made me mad. My father was as smart as his.

Everyone in the neighborhood knew about the secret passage for bootleggers. The only one of the men who came outside was the driver of the car. He washed and waxed the Packard each week and mowed the lawn. Grumble and Mike always stood around and asked the driver questions, but he never answered.

"Interesting," said Clancy. He was good with big words. And we found out later he was a genius. He'd been doing crossword puzzles since he was three, which is why he used big words like "interesting." But as smart as he was, he never figured out how to get the Beans' garage back in place. And he hadn't realized Rudy was a girl. He wasn't perfect.

E L E V E N

Clancy acted bored and grouchy. "What are we going to do today?" We were in the tree house, and the rest of us felt about the same.

"Don't know," said Digger.

"We've been everywhere," I said.

"How about Rudy's clothes chute?" said Digger. Dunster had nailed him again that morning. Whenever that happened he couldn't come up with a good idea.

"We were just there," I said.

"Afraid to go back?" said Digger.

"No."

Rudy licked her cracked lips. "So what are we going to do?"

Clancy stood and looked out over the park. "Ever been across the tracks?"

"No," said Digger. "And we're not interested." Digger was beginning to borrow Clancy's big words.

"Why not?"

"Because we're not supposed to," said Rudy. She stuck her chin out. I pointed. She wiped the saliva off her chin, leaving a dark smear.

"That's right," said Digger. "We're not supposed to."
His face came alive.

"Yeah," I said. And suddenly we were all looking at
each other, chuckling.

"Then it's a deal?" said Clancy.

"Yeah," said Rudy.

"Let's go," said Digger. He was a changed man.

Clancy slid down the trunk, I took the cable swing,
Digger took the second swing, and Rudy grabbed a
level cable, swung out, and dropped to the ground.
Rudy's move was by far the most difficult.

Clancy led out with Digger while Rudy and I followed close behind. We crossed the highway, the first
time for me, and I felt the joy of venturing into the
unknown. I think Rudy felt the same. She acted sillier
than usual.

"Ever find out where babies come from?" said Digger to Clancy. "You know, when you were in the old
neighborhood." Rudy and I ran to catch up. We were
sick of the subject, but we didn't want to miss anything.
Clancy continued chewing on the end of a weed.

"Do we have to talk about that?" said Rudy. She
sounded bored.

"Clancy and I can talk about anything we want."
Digger put his hand on Clancy's shoulder. "Well?"

Clancy rubbed his nose with the back of his wrist.
"The mother lays an egg. And the father drops something to keep the egg warm. Then the mother doesn't
have to sit on the egg like a chicken. They do it like

animals. You know, like dogs."

"No," said Rudy.

"Why not?" said Clancy.

"Disgusting," said Rudy. Another of Clancy's words.

"Well, that's the way it is," he said.

"Horse shit," said Rudy. We argued about it some more, but the idea was too outrageous. Maybe it was Clancy's explanation.

I noticed the clapboard houses, very much like my own. The street was pleasant and tree-lined, but the houses became smaller as we approached the tracks.

We stopped to check things out. Long lines of box cars, flat cars, and gondolas stretched out in both directions, the switchyard for the Monon Railroad. It looked hostile, depressing—everything rusty, splintered, oil-stained; gravel was mixed with a scattering of small chunks of coal.

"What's wrong?" said Clancy.

"We really shouldn't be here," I said.

"Let's try it anyway," said Digger. I was converted for the second time, but I had to give Rudy a shove.

"Do exactly what I do," said Clancy. "And be careful. It's dangerous." He stared at us for a moment, then turned and ran. "Come on!" he shouted.

Clancy ran to the first box car, dropped, crawled, and came out standing up on the opposite side. It didn't look that easy. The trick was to work off the ties and stay out of the gravel.

After two or three attempts, we could actually do it.

And Rudy was fast. I knew she was scared.

When Clancy figured we knew what we were doing, he climbed up the ladder at the end of a box car. We followed, Rudy whimpering all the way. It wasn't the height that bothered her, it was the fear that the car might move. "Shut up," said Digger, but his tone was kind, encouraging. She did. I was proud of her.

We reached the top of the car and crawled along the cat walk to the center and sat down. It was no higher than the tree house, but here it was frightening. There were no weeds below to soften a fall. The sun felt hot on my back; the boards of the cat walk were uncomfortably warm. Clancy shielded his eyes, then pointed to the other side of the tracks. "Over there," he said. "See it?"

"See what?" I said.

"The village."

I looked hard until I saw it. "Oh yeah, interesting."

Across the tracks, in the shadow of two large poplars, was a cluster of huts built of packing cases, chunks of concrete, railroad ties, even sod. And there were roofs of wood and rusty metal. The village looked disorganized, slipshod, yet in a way picturesque.

"Boy, they sure build better huts over here," I said.

"Those aren't for kids," said Clancy. "It's a hobo village. People who live there don't have kids or work or anything. They just do odd jobs and travel."

I could see a fire with men sitting around it. A shabby-looking group, even from that distance. "Why do they live that way?" I said.

"Why not?" said Digger. "Can you smell that coffee?"

"Are you kidding?" I said.

"Smells good to me," said Rudy. It had to be their imaginations. We were too far away. We sat watching them for a long time.

"Why didn't you mention this before?" said Digger.

"I did, but you didn't listen," said Clancy. "And I thought it was too far. Do you want to meet Ernie?"

"Who's Ernie?" said Digger.

"One of the guys who lives there." Clancy glanced at Digger, then at me. "Shall we go?"

"Maybe not," said Rudy.

"Done it a thousand times," said Clancy. He turned and crawled back to the ladder before we had a chance to debate it. Clancy waited below until Rudy hit the gravel, then he took off running as fast as the rails and gravel would allow. We worked hard to stay close behind. On the other side of the tracks, we dropped into a dry ditch filled with cattails. The air smelled like damp soil and decomposition. We were still out of breath.

"Let me do the talking, okay?" said Clancy. No one disagreed. We crawled up the ditch bank and into dense weeds that were well over our heads and so dry they fell away. Grasshoppers, hitting and sometimes clinging, let us know we were invading their territory. The large poplars ahead led us on.

Two small huts built of packing crates stopped us. Clancy looked around. Then motioned for us to follow.

As we passed one of the huts, I looked inside. It was filled with rags, bottles, rusty tools, and an old phonograph with a horn and crank.

Again the path was lost in weeds and bushes. We passed another hut built of sod. Grass grew out of the walls, and the roof was covered with grass and weeds. A dirty piece of red carpet covered the doorway. It looked like it grew out of the ground. The place smelled like our weed huts, with cigars, whiskey, cooked cabbage, and sausage added.

Once in the shadow of the poplars, we entered a large clearing with huts all around. None was tall enough for a man to stand up inside. The most substantial were built of chunks of stacked concrete and looked like they had been there a long time. A fire, centered in the clearing, was surrounded by a dozen men sitting on a log or squatting. They wore filthy flannel shirts or sweaters which looked too hot for a summer day. A black man with a derby wore an unraveling tweed overcoat. Most of them had long, shaggy beards.

A German shepherd jumped up and started toward us, eyeing us like fresh meat. Clancy stopped and we gathered behind him. The black man noticed us. "Come back, Frieda!" he shouted. The dog stopped. The rest of the men were now looking at us, but no one spoke. Finally Clancy stepped forward, knelt down, and patted Frieda on the head. I was impressed.

"Ernie around?" said Clancy. The men looked at each other.

"What do you want him for?" said a large, red-faced man with wide suspenders stretching over a pot belly.

"Just wanted to talk to him," said Clancy. He sounded nervous.

"Well, he ain't here," said the fat man. He coughed and it was deep and raspy.

"Will he be back soon?" said Clancy.

"Beats me," said the fat man.

"Mind if we wait?" Clancy patted the dog one more time, then stood up. I couldn't believe Clancy. I wanted to get out of there. Rudy's eyes said she felt the same.

"Do what you want," the man said, then spit.

"What do you think?" whispered Clancy, his head half turned, talking out of the corner of his mouth.

"Let's get out of here," mumbled Digger. Rudy and I nodded.

"Okay," whispered Clancy. He half nodded to the men as he stepped back, then directed us with his eyes. We followed to the path and soon passed the hut with the red-carpet door. Clancy stopped, then thrust out his arm. I bumped into Digger, and Rudy smacked into me. Two men stood only a short distance away. Rudy sneezed, and the two men looked up. I was shocked. One was the Turk. He acted surprised, almost irritated. He said a few more words to the other short man, then turned and walked away. "What's he doing here?" whispered Digger.

The small man watched the Turk until he disappeared in the weeds, then he turned and walked toward us. He wore old corduroy knickers and a leather golfer's cap.

"Hi, Ernie," said Clancy. I was surprised. The man didn't act like he recognized Clancy until he was standing right in front of him.

"What are you doing here?" said Ernie. His smile disappeared. "I thought I told you never to come here again."

"These are different guys," said Clancy. "I thought . . ."

"Well, don't think," he said. "I told you before this is no place for kids." Ernie's nose was only inches away from Clancy's. "We've had some bad men go through lately. It isn't safe."

"Okay," said Clancy. He stepped back. "We'll go."

"This minute," said Ernie. He reached out, touched my shoulder, and gave me a shove, then walked with us until we reached the tracks. "Be careful," he said. "And hurry."

"See you," said Clancy over his shoulder.

"I hope not," shouted Ernie. "And don't ever come with that girl." He pointed at Rudy.

Clancy glared at Rudy. "Let's go," he said. "Here comes a brakeman." I couldn't see who he was pointing at, but again we were running across the tracks, struggling to keep our footing.

Clancy slipped under the first car, and I followed. We crawled under another, then another. When I crawled out from beneath the last car, I could see our side of the tracks. A thrilling sight. We were safe at last. We ran and skipped and tumbled the rest of the way home.

T W E L V E

The evening my father announced the trip to Utah, I was stunned. So was Mary Lou. He always spoke of "the mountains" as if there were some magic there, but mountains had no meaning for me. All I could think of was leaving warm summer days, the monkey tree, the park, the forest preserve.

He talked about a trip for several years, but business hadn't been good, and it was postponed. This time our new black Ford made the difference. He wanted my mother to meet his family. She had never been West before. For him it was a kind of pilgrimage, a return to the center. He listened to our pleas and pretended he understood, but I knew we were doomed. It was all tied up with being Mormon, but I had enough of that on Sundays. Church was a pain, an interruption. Sundays were ruined by two trips in heavy traffic into Chicago. The meetings were long and boring. I would have traded in a minute with my Catholic cousins. They could walk to church and be out in less than an hour. So it was in Latin. Once Mass was over, they were through for the day. Mary Lou and I never defended the faith with our cousins. There was no contest. To be Mormon was to suffer.

Father was the only one who really liked to travel. Mother lived by schedule. It gave her life meaning. Monday, wash day. Tuesday, ironing. Wednesday, bridge club, Thursday, P.T.A., and Friday housecleaning. Interrupting her schedule was like changing the course of a river. She worried about keeping Mary Lou and me on oatmeal and cod liver oil while traveling. Managing our nutrition was her religion.

Monday morning I walked in the kitchen and found Mary Lou spooning pictures in her oatmeal. Except for my father's being there, everything seemed normal.

"Better hurry," said my father. "We're leaving in half an hour."

"Where are we going?" I said.

"It's a surprise."

"We're not going on a trip?" said Mary Lou.

"You heard me," he said. "It's a surprise."

I looked at Mary Lou. She shrugged, then stood and walked to the sink with her bowl of oatmeal.

"You're not through yet," snapped my mother, darting through.

"I thought we were in a hurry," said Mary Lou. She stomped her foot, then returned to the table. I made a face. She stuck out her tongue. Monday mornings were always bad. Too close to Sundays.

I went outside and noticed luggage stacked on the car's back bumper. "We're not going on a trip!" I said to myself. It was too late. My father, right behind, deposited me in the back seat. Mary Lou was crying when Mother pushed her in beside me and locked the door. It was as simple as that. We were being kidnapped. By our parents.

We drove off, and Mary Lou and I refused to talk, despite my father's efforts. We looked out at open fields whizzing by and occasionally whimpered loud enough to be heard above the rush of hot air pouring in. Not a happy start.

Several hours passed before Mary Lou insisted she had to go to the bathroom. I said I was also desperate, anything to escape the back seat.

"We have to find a Conoco station," said my mother. It was the only gasoline chain with rest rooms that passed her white glove inspection. So we had to wait, gambling on permanent organ damage.

Mother sat in front with the road maps, trying to act as navigator. She calculated distances and made projections for arrival times. "It'll be nice to pass through Phoenix," she said.

My father looked straight ahead. "We won't get close to Phoenix."

"Oh," she said. "I wasn't holding the map straight." She bent over the map, squinting. "The next town we come to is Omaha."

"Des Moines," he said.

"Didn't we just cross the Missouri River?"

"The Mississippi," he said.

The mosquito-splattered car climbed, then descended the roller-coaster countryside of Iowa, following the thin black line of asphalt that shimmered in radiating heat. The sun was blinding as it descended slowly in the west, and the back seat was unbearably hot. Our heads hung limply out the window as if disconnected, our bodies dehydrating in the wind. My mother continued to discuss all the cities we would not be visiting.

The trip took a full three days, and we came out of the mountains east of Salt Lake City just in time to see the sunset over the Great Salt Lake. It was orange, like a sea of hot metal, and the lights of the city began to fill the lush, green valley. Mountains to the west, purple in the fading light, gave a strong sense of enclosure, security. The air was cool and fresh. I noticed tears in my father's eyes and sensed, if only in a limited way, what he was feeling. By the time we arrived at the city center, the flood-lit spires of the temple were ascending jewel-like above the black-green foliage. We stopped and looked at the temple for a long time.

We stayed that night with an aunt and uncle who had no children, which meant that Mary Lou and I received a lot of unwanted attention. My uncle said I looked just like my father and Mary Lou like her mother. I was flattered, proud to look like my father, but Mary Lou didn't look anything like my mother. I loved my mother.

The following day was Sunday, and my father announced we were going to a family reunion. "What's that?" said Mary Lou.

"It's a picnic for the family."

I nudged Mary Lou. "More relatives," I said. Her eyes went up. It was the kind of thing you could expect from a vacation.

When we arrived at Liberty Park, it was filled with people crowded under the cool shade of pine trees, cottonwoods, pavilions, and a tent someone had pitched. A soft wind stirred the white fluff from the cottonwoods, and the smell of fried chicken was everywhere. My uncle took off to find the Bradshaws, then called for us to follow. My father ran ahead. When the rest of us arrived at a large pavilion, he was hugging old ladies and trying to talk to everyone at once. I was hugged and kissed by so many grinning strangers I wanted to run. They were a strange looking group and I wondered about the whole idea of relatives. I hadn't really accepted Mary Lou yet.

It took some time before the hugging stopped, but finally Mary Lou and I broke free and went in search of something better to do. A girl cousin, who took a liking to Mary Lou, led the way. Her name was Cleo. She had to repeat the name three times before I got it. Coming from a group like that, I wasn't surprised. My Polish cousins had more respectable names.

But Cleo was all right. She was small and springy. She never walked, she skipped. And she was fast. I had to run just to keep up with her.

We passed a large tent brimming with Hinckleys and they didn't look that great either. We passed Jorgensons and Farrels and I don't know how many others. It was good that I saw them. I felt better about the Bradshaws.

But all the families had these funny looking banners with an ugly shape. "What's that?" I said, then pointed.

"It's a family tree, said Cleo. She exhaled, impatient to move on.

"A what?" said Mary Lou. She squinted.

"A family tree," said Cleo.

"What's it for?" I said.

"To show all the people in the family," she said.

I looked harder at the black, grotesque form with tentacles and suddenly understood what she was talking about. The tree had names written in the branches. Cleo explained that some were living and some were dead. That made it even worse. The ugly tree belonged in a haunted forest. It was exactly the kind of thing you could expect from a family reunion. Later I saw the deformed tree in a nightmare with gnarled branches of dead relatives crying out as the wind forced them into motion.

"We've got one for the Bradshaws," said Cleo. "Want to see it. My name's on it. Maybe yours is, too." I looked at Mary Lou.

"No thanks," she said. Every once in a while Mary Lou showed some sense.

Eventually we found some swings and a slippery slide, and even though they were dull, it was better than anything else we had seen in a long time. When we returned to the reunion, everyone was sitting around listening to an old lady with thick glasses tell how my grandfather walked to Salt Lake Valley in 1847. I kept glancing at the family tree. Sometimes it looked like it moved. I wondered whether my name was on it but didn't really want to find out.

I met my grandmother at the reunion, but the following three days were spent at her white clapboard cottage. It was snuggled into a peach orchard just north of the city. She was round and sturdy, with gray hair and black eyes that held you when she spoke. Her voice was deep, and she chuckled at everything I said. And I was surprised at how well she spoke English. I thought grandparents spoke other languages.

My father was unusually happy. He cut kindling for the wood stove, baked bread, cooked meals, which he never did at home. And he talked from early morning until well into the night. I think my mother enjoyed it also, but she didn't say much.

Fortunately our cousin Cleo was staying with Grandmother while her mother had a baby. She was full of ideas. Whatever we did, we somehow sensed it was against the rules. We started out in the orchard diverting water from the irrigation ditch into a series of small canals we dug. My grandmother spotted us. "Never waste water in the desert," she scolded.

Cleo was hardly intimidated. We followed her to the barbed wire fence surrounding the orchard and slipped underneath to rest behind an old water trough. Cleo looked around. "You know who lives in the big house over there?" She poked her head up and pointed. I half stood and saw a large, half painted house with four white columns supporting a two-story porch. Shabby. Slipshod. I ducked down again.

"No," I whispered. "Who?"

"Polygamists," said Cleo. She stuck out her chin to let us know this was privileged information.

"What did you say?" said Mary Lou.

"Polygamists," repeated Cleo. "They have lots of wives and a hundred kids."

"Where are all the kids?" I said. I could hear voices from somewhere. It sounded like the park in the morning.

"Look," she said. She stretched and pointed. "Over there."

I peaked around the corner of the trough. There, behind a large barn with a precarious lean, was a crowd of kids. One group was romping in a haystack, another played tag, while two older boys threw a rubber ball at a bent basketball hoop. Their clothes were worn and ill-fitting, but they were having a good time.

"Ever play with them?" said Mary Lou.

"Oh, no," said Cleo. "They can't play with anyone. They don't even go to school. Their mothers teach them at home."

"Wait a minute," I said. "They don't go to school?"

"That's right." It sounded too good to be true.

"Why don't they?" said Mary Lou.

"Because they're illegal." Cleo nodded.

"What does that mean?" I said.

"I don't know," she said. "But they have to hide because they're wicked."

"Who says they're wicked?" said Mary Lou.

"Everybody. They don't even dare go to church. They stay home and have their own church." It sounded better all the time.

Grandmother's tiny kitchen smelled like baked bread and burnt wood from the stove. And that evening we had beef stew and talked about the polygamists. I wanted to know everything. My father explained that Mormons once practiced polygamy but gave it up. I was disappointed. Then he said that in the old days it wasn't considered wicked and the kids had to go to school and church. I figured that pretty well removed all the advantages.

T H I R T E E N

As we headed north two days later, my father informed us that we were headed for the Mormon temple in Logan. He said what happened there was very serious, and Mary Lou and I were expected to be unusually good. We fought the entire way.

We drove to a grassy knoll overlooking the city of Logan and looked down on the temple—a gray stone building with white towers. My parents had already been married, but a temple wedding was different. They had to go through a special ritual before the ceremony. It seemed kind of silly, but I didn't say anything. Mary Lou and I played out on the front lawn of the temple for over an hour. Finally an old woman dressed like a maid called us in and made us put on white clothes—shoes, socks, underwear, the works. Mary Lou cried when she decided the white dress didn't fit, and I was mad because the lady wouldn't leave when I changed clothes. She was a busybody, a lot like Mrs. Bean. I liked her even less when she wet my hair and slicked it down with a comb.

Mary Lou and I were taken down a long hall, then

into a room with a white altar centered under a glass chandelier. It was fancy, like the living rooms of mansions back home, but nothing like a church. My father and mother were dressed in white and waiting for us. It all seemed very solemn until my mother started to giggle. Then Mary Lou pointed at me and my father joined in. When I looked in the large mirror across the room, I understood. The old woman had parted my hair on the wrong side. Even I started laughing.

A man in a white dress suit entered the room and stood by the doorway waiting until we quieted down. Then he smiled and shook hands with my father. "Would you please kneel at the altar," he said, then made sure we all took our proper places. It was a lot better organized than anything Digger ever worked up.

"That's good" the man said. "Let me just take a moment to explain to you children that your parents are being married for eternity, and you in turn are being sealed to them. Now, how long is eternity?" He looked at Mary Lou.

"It's forever," she said. When I heard that I felt sick inside. Forever was okay for my parents. But Mary Lou? The man proceeded with the ceremony, but I didn't hear much. I was thinking about being stuck with Mary Lou. Forever.

Later that afternoon, on the way out of Logan, my father announced he'd saved the best part of the trip until last. He liked surprises, but our idea of a good surprise didn't coincide.

"What are we going to do?" I said. I figured I might as well get it over with.

"I want to go home," said Mary Lou.

"Guess," said my father, paying no attention to her.

"I don't know," I said.

"Who cares?" said Mary Lou. She was pouting and flipping the strap by the back window.

"We're going to Yellowstone Park," he said.

Silence.

He turned and looked at us, then returned to Mother. "Guess they're not interested." Mary Lou exhaled loudly and looked out the window.

"What's so nifty about Yellowstone Park?" I said.

We entered the park the following morning and drove for miles. And hours. It was huge, not my idea of a park at all. We passed some deer and moose grazing, but we didn't see a single bear. There were a lot of places with steam and smoke coming out of the ground, but after awhile we got tired of that. At noon my father finally stopped at a camping area. Mary Lou and I had been in the car too long.

After a picnic lunch, we started off on a trail that led to a bubbling pool my father wanted to see. I still had a half-eaten apple in my hand. There were sulfur springs along the way, and the trail was covered with steam. I walked ahead until I was stopped by a pool of boiling muck at the side of the path. It was the ugliest thing I had ever seen and smelled ten times worse than a steel mill or oil refinery. Sulfur steam covered the path ahead.

"Is this it?" I said.

My father pointed. "There's a bigger one ahead." I walked through the mist and passed a pool that smelled even worse. Large gray bubbles burst and released rancid smoke. I walked on, and once in the clear I decided to finish off the apple. After the first bite, I knew something was wrong. My tongue felt a space, then my finger confirmed a tooth was gone. But where? I dropped to the ground and looked around. It was worth big money from the tooth fairy.

I finally spotted the tooth projecting from the apple and tried to pry it loose. That's when I spotted the bear. A large, brown bear, walking toward me. Only a few feet away. I looked back for my father. He wasn't there. The bear stopped in front of me, then rolled back on his rump and pawed the air. His paws were sandpaper rough, his claws worn. Drool hung from his opened mouth exposing disgusting, brown teeth. His beady eyes looked anxious. I dropped the half-finished apple at his feet. He rolled forward, snatched up the apple, rolled back, and chucked it in his mouth like it was nothing more than a peanut. He didn't even chew it. One swallow and it was gone. So was my tooth.

He pawed the air again, making it clear he wanted more. I was so close I could smell his breath. "Hold still," whispered my father. His hand was on my shoulder. He dropped a Baby Ruth bar at my feet. The bear pitched forward and tore at the paper wrapper. My father pulled me back until we were some distance away. Mother and Mary Lou joined us along with two older couples. The men took pictures of the bear eating the candy bar, or rather swallowing it. "He ate my tooth," I said.

"Your what?" My father picked me up and held me.

"My tooth," I whimpered, then I started to cry. I would have continued if the bear hadn't passed by. Everyone stepped out of the way. Soon he was enveloped in mist, and seconds later we heard a woman scream. Then a man yelled, "Help!" The bear must have scared them in the mist. Everyone laughed. It made me feel better, if only for a moment.

It took some time explaining to my father that the tooth first went into the apple, which in turn went into the bear. When he finally understood, he burst out laughing. Mary Lou and Mother weren't that polite either. Before I got emotional again, he slipped me a dime and said he'd work it out with the tooth fairy.

We continued up the path, but all we found was a bigger pool of gray stewing muck and huge clouds of stinking mist. We visited Old Faithful and Yellowstone Falls, steaming lakes and more pools of bubbling goo, but nothing equalled meeting the bear. I couldn't wait to tell Clancy, Digger, and Rudy, even though I'd have to omit some of the details. They wouldn't want to know I cried.

Three mind-numbing days, trapped in the back

seat with Mary Lou, had to be faced again, and I was so depressed I was speechless. In the back seat, Mary Lou fingered a line in the upholstery. Territory was established.

I looked at the motel's white clapboard cottages as my father backed out the car.

"Well, what do you think?" he said. It wasn't a question. He was looking for praise.

"About what?" said Mary Lou. A chill was in her voice.

"The trip," said my father. He was still smiling.

"It was very nice," I said.

"Yes," said Mary Lou. "It was nice."

"Good," said my father. He turned, and the car moved slowly out on the highway.

"It was stupid," mouthed Mary Lou.

My father saw her in the rear-view mirror. He shook his head. Mother was convinced Mary Lou was almost perfect, but I sensed my father was a little suspicious. I didn't think the trip was stupid. I thought it was confusing. It was difficult to sort things out. Even I didn't like the bleeding Jesus in my cousin's church, but the image of the family tree was no improvement. And there was the strange ceremony in the temple with everyone dressed in white. It was too nice. Dull nice. I wondered whether I would ever fit in anywhere. In Indiana I felt too Mormon. In Utah I felt too Polish.

My mother began studying the maps and looked as

confused as ever. "What's the next town?" she said.

"Rock Springs, Wyoming," said my father.

"We better stop at a gas station for new maps," she said. The word "stop" always unnerved my father.

"What in heaven's name for?" he said. The windows were down, the wind was blowing through, and at last we were making good time.

"Well, I can hardly use these." She tossed the stack of maps off to the side. "What am I supposed to do? Read them backwards?"

My father drove off to the side and braked. The car was enveloped in a cloud of dust. He threw his head back and roared. There were tears in his eyes by the time Mary Lou and I caught on. Mother was happy at her success. We sat there laughing, repeating the punch line over and over again.

Three times a day we stopped at the central cafe on the main street of whatever town we were passing through. The cafes all looked alike both outside and in. The waitresses wore the same outfits and looked like they were all related. Even the menus were the same.

By the third day, Mother had even stopped reading the maps. She sensed we were approaching home. Despite her remark the day before about Kansas City, she caught the error before my father had a chance to comment.

As the afternoon wore on, and the heat increased, and my father admitted there were still another four hours to drive, Mary Lou and I turned on each other like caged badgers. We had started out the morning singing, then my father had told stories about his childhood, but the heat and boredom of the afternoon had long since drained off the friendly mood. Slowly we became four separate beings attempting to survive the proximity.

When the punching and clawing became too much, my father's large hand appeared out of nowhere to separate us. Eventually we sat back in our corners and glowered.

I thought about Digger, Rudy, and Clancy and all the fun I had missed. They didn't even know I was leaving. Now I was coming back and all I had done was visit relatives.

I looked out at dull, flat fields of corn bordered by power lines and dirt roads. A disgusting sound slowly worked its way into my awareness. I turned to Mary Lou. She was chewing bubble gum.

"Where'd you get that?" I said.

"None of your business," she snapped, then turned and looked out the window.

"May I have some?" I said, knowing what the answer would be. She wrinkled her nose and shook her head. I would have attacked, but I was too hot and tired. She blew a big bubble and looked cross-eyed across it. I watched until it collapsed. "Bet I could blow a bigger one," I said.

"So could I," she said.

"I'll bet a dime," I said. She thought for a moment.

"Okay." She tried another, but it burst.

"Give you one more try," I said.

She eyed me warily, then tried again. The bubble grew larger and larger. Her eyes showed overconfidence as the bubble expanded. When it broke, and it was magnificent, it covered her eyes, lashes, and half her face. I burst out laughing. Mother spun around and screamed. It was a perfect way to end the trip. She never got the dime.

I heard the call of a morning dove when I woke up. I was free. I even accepted oatmeal without complaint. But I questioned the whole idea of parental fealty. If friends had come up with a lousy idea like the trip, then put me through the pain of it, I would have had nothing more to do with them. I stared at my mother sitting across from me in her curlers and flowered housecoat. I wondered how she and my father could have been so presumptuous. I stood, walked to the garbage can under the sink, dumped the remainder of oatmeal, then ran out the back door, pretending I didn't hear my mother calling.

I ran, skipped, and tumbled, but when I arrived at the monkey tree no one was there. I wanted to celebrate. I climbed to the tree house, then even higher to a large limb, and viewed the familiar surroundings. Two kids were on the swings at the park. Mrs. Becker was hanging out wash. The driver of the black Packard was mowing the lawn across the street. Nothing had changed. It was all there just as I had tried to recall during those punishing days in the car.

Finally I saw Digger walking slowly toward me with Blackie tagging along behind. He sat down at the base of the tree and proceeded to remove bark from a twig. I quickly broke off a dead limb, aimed, and let it fall. It hit his shoulder and he jumped to his feet, dancing around like a boxer. He was looking for Dunster.

A big smile swallowed his tense face once he spotted me. "You're back!" he shouted.

"Yep!" I slid down the trunk to the tree house platform, jumped for the cable, swung down, and dropped beside him. "Old Blackie didn't hit Bean's this morning," I said. "I was watching for you."

"I know." He frowned.

"Why not?"

"Dunster," he said. "She's on to that."

"Oh," I said, then looked around. "Where is everybody?"

"Here!" screamed Clancy. He jumped out from behind the trunk, grinning like a ghoul. I jumped back and Clancy gave me the old horse laugh.

"Funny," I said.

Rudy came strolling up. "Hi," she said.

I could tell she was glad to see me. I nodded, and she slapped me on the shoulder.

"How was the trip?" said Clancy.

"Interesting," I said.

"Come on," said Clancy. He knew I was lying.

"Okay," I said. "It was boring."

"What did you do?" said Digger.

"Sat in the car and visited relatives."

"Is that all? " said Clancy.

"Oh yeah. My parents got married."

"Married?" said Digger. "Weren't they married?"

"They got married in the temple," I said. "For eternity."

"What's that?" lisped Rudy. I noticed she'd lost another tooth.

"It means you get married forever," I said.

"That's a long time," said Clancy. He was picking at a scab on his elbow.

"My father wouldn't like that," said Rudy.

"Boy, I guess," said Digger. He gave me a knowing glance and Rudy saw it. Digger shrugged.

"That's all you did?" said Clancy.

I tried to explain about the family reunion and the family tree, but they weren't interested. It was probably the way I explained it. Then I told them about the polygamists and their children who didn't have to go to school and they really liked that. And when I told them about the bear eating my tooth, they were awed.

"You mean the bear just up and ate your tooth?" said Rudy. She was grinning, and I couldn't take my eyes off the missing tooth.

"No, he ate the apple," I said. "And the tooth was in it."

"Wonder what happened to the tooth?" said Digger.

"Figure it out," said Clancy.

"Probably just . . ." said Digger, outlining the digestive flow with both hands and ending with a gross sound. Everyone laughed. I repeated the story, and they enjoyed it as much the second time. It was great to be back.

F O U R T E E N

School was going to start the following Monday and all we did was gripe. By late morning we couldn't stand each other, but after lunch we were in a better mood.

"We can't just sit around," said Digger.

"Then think of something," said Rudy.

I thought Digger was going to paste her. He looked off. "All right, dammit. Let's go to your house and hit the clothes chute."

"Yeah," said Clancy. "Why not."

I dropped the dried grasshopper I was taking apart and stood up. "Let's go before we all go crazy."

Digger dove at me, and we fell to the ground, laughing. He jumped up, pushed me back down, then took off running. "Last one there is a jackass!" he shouted.

I passed Digger and Rudy just before they arrived in front of her house. "What's wrong with them?" said Rudy, still out of breath. She pointed at two girls coming out the back yard gate. One had her head in her hands, the other had red eyes, and wet cheeks.

"Who are they?" said Digger.

"Beats me," said Rudy.

The girls passed us.

"What's wrong?" I said.

The first one ran off sobbing, but the second one stopped. "That . . . that lady in there . . ." She pointed. "That lady screamed at us."

"Geez," said Digger. "Is that all?" The girl's face wrinkled up—she started to cry. Then she ran off.

Digger cupped his hands and shouted. "She's always like that!" He turned to Rudy. "Your mom's on one today?"

"Naw," said Rudy. "She's okay."

Digger pushed the gate open and walked into the back yard. The day was hot, low-hanging clouds pressed down like a wet overcoat. Rain was on its way. Perhaps that's what made us testy. We followed Digger into the back door and scrambled up the half flight of stairs. Clancy had led yesterday, it was Digger's turn today. But Digger stopped cold when he saw Rudy's mother. The rest of us crashed into him. She stood at the kitchen sink barefoot, her hair bound in a kerchief. Without false teeth, her cheeks fell into her mouth. "You mess my house, I bust your head!" she yelled.

"Yes ma'am," said Digger. "We'll be awful careful." He was so polite it made you sick. Rudy's mother gave us a long, unforgiving look.

The clothes chute was great. In no time we were screaming, pushing, tripping, and finally tumbling through the chute, then racing back for another try. Even Blackie fell down the chute. Rudy's mother walked into the living room and yelled, "No running!" each time we passed. All things considered, it was about normal.

Digger and I were on our way through the dining room when Rudy's mother hollered, "Stop! Right now!" She was dusting her favorite blue and green porcelain lamp with bear claws and a large shade with spangles. Digger and I stopped.

She threw down her dust rag, screamed something in Slovak, then came after us. I stopped, but Digger kept going. She lunged at Digger, missed, then took a swipe at me. She missed but lost her balance. The lamp slipped from her fingers. Fell to the floor. Broke into a million pieces. She looked down, then let out an ungodly shriek. We scattered like rats from a nest. Clancy and Rudy ran for the clothes chute. Digger and Blackie (I'm not sure who went first) raced through the kitchen, down the back stairs, and went out the screen door without opening it. The torn screen made a ripping sound.

I was cut off from the clothes chute and the back door. I ran back to the living room and dove behind the couch. She was right behind. She threw herself on the couch, and I could hear it creak as she reached down the back side, but I was out the front and on my way. I ran to the kitchen, down the stairs, and through the hole in the screen door.

"Over here!" shouted Digger. I stopped, but couldn't see him. Rudy's mother came out of the screen door screaming.

"Come on," shouted Digger. I spotted him by the gate, but it was too late. Rudy's mother had me cut off. She took after Digger, but he jumped through the gate and closed it. I ran to the wire fence and tried to roll over. The top wire caught me and threw me back to the ground.

I jumped up and ran in a wide circle, looking for another escape. Rudy's mother stood in the middle of the lawn, waiting. A ladder leaned against the eave of the house. My only hope. I faked a run for the gate. Rudy's mother lunged. Missed. I turned, ran back to the ladder and scrambled up.

Once on the roof I looked down, and there she was. Feet spread apart. Fists clenched. Surely she wouldn't, but she did. She started up the ladder. The giant, crazy lady was coming after me.

I looked around. There was only one thing to do. I ran up to the ridge, then down the other side and dropped to the lawn below. I hit, rolled, then sprang to my feet and ran. I caught up with Digger about a half block away and only then dared to look back. There on the ridge of the roof stood a wild, screaming figure. We ran for home.

Clancy and Rudy were forgotten until I reached the safety of my room, then I wondered whether they had escaped. I found Clancy at the monkey tree after dinner. He told how he and Rudy went down the clothes chute, then out the back door while Rudy's mother was on the roof. "Is Rudy's mother crazy?" he said.

"I think she was upset," I said.

"Maybe we shouldn't go back for awhile. You know. It was great and all. And I'm not afraid."

"I could wait for awhile," I said.

"We won't have time anyway. School starts Monday."

"Don't remind me." I was so depressed I couldn't enjoy the rest of the evening.

Sunday after church I couldn't find anyone at the park or monkey tree. I went to Clancy's, then Digger's, but neither one was home. I even went to Rudy's house, hoping to find her outside. I didn't dare go up and knock on the door. Then I spotted Rudy's mother at the side of the house mowing the lawn. She saw me. She called in a nice voice, but I pretended not to hear. She called again and motioned for me to come closer. I approached her, staying on the opposite side of the fence.

"You want to play with Rudy?" she said. Her voice was warm and friendly. I had never seen her like this before.

"Is she at home?" I said.

She raised a hand to her mouth and called. I tried to think of something to say. "Maybe we forget what happen, yes?" She smiled and I could see her false teeth. She looked a lot better. I waited. "I mean about you break my lamp," she said. She reached across the fence and tried to pat my hand.

I stepped back. "I didn't break your lamp."
"Maybe we just forget?" she said.
I nodded, still looking at her ugly feet.

F I F T E E N

Monday was a perfect day about to be wasted in the hot, dead air of a classroom. My first day in the second grade. I knew the routine. I was expected to sit in this dull room with desks surrounded on three sides by green blackboards, and the fourth with book shelves and windows too high to see out. The playhouse, the musical instruments, the building blocks from kindergarten were now only a memory. Books, charts, and maps took their place. It was deadly serious. And there was a whole year ahead.

Familiar faces from the year before showed no signs of panic. Some girls were even laughing. Didn't they understand? Even Willie Lamb was smiling. I was disgusted. I could see how girls could be taken in, but a boy? Anyone with sense could see it was a conspiracy.

Wally Bentz came strolling in with a big grin on his face. "Hi, Wally," I said. I never liked Wally, he always played with girls.

"Hi," he said, then plopped down in a desk and looked around. If anyone fit in, it was old Wally.

I heard my name and seat assignment but didn't

111

move until Clancy shoved me in the right direction. "Sit down," he whispered.

"Where?" I said. He pointed. I fell into a seat, listening to the names as they were read off. It was clear Clancy was also bought off. I was alone. All I could think about was the monkey tree, the smell of cut grass, the feel of the warm sun on my back.

The second grade teacher, Miss Griswald, known as Grizzly Bear on the playground, was old, her voice raspy. She always had bad breath, and her small, beady eyes, made even smaller by thick glasses, saw everything. She moved silently through the classroom, wrapped in a cloud of moist, sour air. I knew when she stood behind me before I heard her heavy breathing.

"Attention!" she shouted. It was her favorite word. "I'm glad to see all of you here this morning. I know we're going to have a wonderful year." She attempted a smile. "First, I should explain a few things. I like to do the same subjects at the same time every day. That way we don't miss anything. First thing is spelling. Then reading. We try to get through those two before recess. Afterwards it's grammar. When you come back from lunch we do our math. And after recess, if you're good, I'll read a story." She attempted another smile that strained her mouth. I looked at Clancy, and he was listening like she was saying something important.

We started right in with spelling. I was not good at spelling. Or reading. Or grammar. Or math. I was a total flop.

I knew the alphabet in order, but when the letters formed words I found them confusing. Z and N, w and m, even b and d were hard to tell apart. The year before I spent most of the time looking out the window, wishing I were somewhere else.

That night I had a nightmare about old Grizzly Bear. She appeared as a fur-bearing monster with huge fangs extending well below the lip, stalking me with a second grade reader. I was convinced she hated children—all children—particularly me. The tortures of school work gave her life purpose. She was the cause of my failure. Dream and reality often blended into one.

Why hadn't Digger warned me? He was a year ahead and surely had had old Grizzly Bear. How did he make it through? Clancy was no help either. Grizzly Bear found out how smart he was and fawned over him. Whenever I complained, Digger and Clancy just shrugged it off. I was trapped. There was nothing to look forward to but recess, lunch, three-fifteen, and Saturdays. I thought I would go mad.

When the first weekend arrived, it was a celebration. I could look forward to an entire day without seeing, hearing, or smelling old Grizzly Bear. We met at the park early. Rudy was there, Digger was full of ideas, and Clancy was agreeable. Suddenly it was summer again and everything was right. We crowded the day with the monkey tree, the pickle factory, the forest preserve. We even swiped some grapes from the Turk's back yard, but they were still green and sour.

That evening my mother informed me we had to hurry with dinner. Mary Lou was to be in a dance recital at a theater before a large crowd. I had been to recitals before. And could think of nothing worse except school. I'd even take church. Who could enjoy pale, skinny girls, dressed in odd, ill-fitting costumes, lined up but failing unison, clicking away like mechanical midgets? I nibbled on a piece of chocolate cake, stalling for time.

Mary Lou appeared in the doorway and I was struck dumb. Her costume. She was supposed to be a dragon-fly, but who could have guessed? Long curls stuffed into a skin-tight headdress forced deep wrinkles in her forehead. Two long wires were intended as antennae. A framework of wire, covered with cellophane, didn't begin to look like wings. Her dress, a white slippery material, was full of wrinkles, and two bandaids stood out on her bowed legs. White anklets sagged over single-strap dancing shoes. This was a costume?

I fell to the floor howling. Then I sat up and pointed. She stood in silence until her face wrinkled up. She spun around and fled down the hall, sobbing. The bathroom door clicked shut.

My mother came in, glared at me, then rushed down the hall and knocked on the bathroom door. No one answered. "Come out!" she shouted. "Stop this silliness!"

She waited. "Mary Lou. We're going to be late!" No answer. "Mary Lou!" Still no answer.

I laughed and rolled on the floor. "Stop it!" screamed my mother. She raced back to the kitchen and gave me a swat on the rump. "See what you've done?"

"What's all the fuss?" shouted my father. He pounded on the bathroom door. "Come out, Mary Lou! Come out this minute!"

A small voice came from the other side. "I can't come out." I tiptoed into the hall to hear better.

"Why not?" he shouted.

"Because I look like a moron."

"You don't look like a moron." He looked at the floor. "You look like a butterfly."

"Dragon fly," whispered my mother. That really cracked me up. I burst out laughing. My father's hand covered my mouth.

"Then why is he laughing?" she cried.

"Because he doesn't understand what you're supposed to be." He continued glaring at me.

"I know what she's supposed to be," I said. The hand returned.

"What did he say?" she cried.

"He said you look like a butterfly."

"No he didn't," she cried. The three of us stood looking at each other.

"All right!" he shouted, then shook the door. It must have frightened her because she was silent after that. He ran to the basement and returned with a screwdriver and pliers. It took several minutes to take the door off its hinges.

Mother gasped when she saw Mary Lou. Her eyes were red, the rouge on her cheeks was streaked from tears, and lipstick was smeared across her chin and covered the back of her hand. Mother started to cry.

"Will everyone please calm down?" my father said. He grabbed Mary Lou and ran to the car.

"We'll have to punish you for this," my mother shouted. "You'll have to stay home alone." She grabbed her purse and raced out the door and didn't even notice my phony act of looking hurt.

This was the most rewarding punishment I ever received. I went out with Digger, Rudy, and Clancy, swiped apples, stayed out way after dark, and still beat them home. I figured I'd have to wait a long time before things lined up that well again.

Back in school Monday, the punishing week began. By Tuesday I was beside myself, and by Wednesday I was considering running away. I mentioned it to Bernie Heifitz. For some reason I was walking home with him, and at first he sounded sympathetic.

"When I get bored, I think of something I like to do," he said. "Then it isn't so bad." Bernie did well in school. I didn't believe for a minute he was ever miserable. But it sounded like a good idea. Immediately Christmas popped into my head. A toy fire engine. A sock full of hard candy. A Christmas tree filled with shiny balls and colored lights.

"What are you going to ask for at Christmas?" I said.

Bernie gave me a funny look. "What's Christmas?"

"Come on Bernie, Christmas."

"So? What's that?"

I stopped and looked hard at him. "I thought you were trying to help?"

"I was," he said.

"I asked you what you're getting for Christmas."

"Yeah, and I asked you, 'What's Christmas?'"

"Come on, Bernie. Don't act stupid."

"I'm not. Just curious." He set his jaw in that way that always irritated me.

"I don't believe you," I said, then kicked a black stink bug off to the side. "If you don't know about Christmas . . ." I turned and spit.

"Never heard of it," he said. Bernie was a lousy actor.

I wanted to kill him. The day had already been bad enough with old Grizzly Bear. "You're not funny, Bernie. You know that?" Then I said the meanest thing I could think of. "I hope you don't get a thing for Christmas."

"Why should I?" he said. "I don't even know what it is."

"That does it." I started walking fast. "Let's not talk about it anymore." And we never did.

When I told Digger and Clancy what happened,

they didn't know what to think. "Sometimes Bernie's a little strange," Digger said. Even with his doubt about Santa Claus, Digger liked Christmas.

That night at dinner, I told my father what Bernie had said. He took a long time explaining why Jews didn't celebrate Christmas. And that their religion was older than Christianity.

"You mean they can never have a Christmas tree?"

"Never," he said. "But they have other celebrations." Then he mentioned the "Gentiles Only" signs on picnic areas and campgrounds that kept Jews out.

"You mean Bernie's family can't go everywhere?"

"That's right," he said. "And it's wrong. People should accept everyone. That's what this country is all about."

We talked about the Jewish religion for a long time. When we finished, I was still confused. I wondered why people as smart as adults hadn't settled such things a long time ago.

The following day was grim as usual, but afterward we had a great time playing tag in the trees. I returned home a little late and was surprised that dinner wasn't ready. This had never happened before. My mother and father were sitting at the kitchen table and she was angry about something.

"Where have you been?" she said.

"What's wrong?"

"Everything," she said. "Everything."

"Calm down," said my father.

My mother folded her arms and gave me an icy stare. "What did you tell your friends about our trip?"

"I don't know," I said. "They didn't seem that interested."

"Did you tell them about the wedding?" said my father. "In the temple?"

"Sure, why not?" I said.

"Then both of them did," my mother said. Mary Lou sat in the corner looking guilty.

"Isn't that what happened?" I said.

"Sit down," he said. I dropped into a chair.

"It's not that simple," he said. "First, it went through your mother's bridge club. Now it's all over the neighborhood. Everyone has the wrong idea."

"I don't know why," I said.

"Dummy," Mary Lou said. She made a face. I stuck out my tongue.

"That's enough," he said. He waited for us to calm down. "People don't understand. And it's not that easy to explain. It's going to take some time to clear this up."

I shrugged.

My mother pushed back her chair and stood up. "I don't want people to think we've . . ." She walked out of the room.

"Think what?" I said.

My father shook his head and rubbed his eyes. "Just don't say anymore about it, understand? Even if your friends ask questions."

"That's easy," I said. "They're not interested."

I never found out exactly what happened, but Dunster's mother was the one who spread the word. It was good my friends weren't the source. Mary Lou must have made a big production out of it, like she always did, and it went from there. My mother said it took a couple of months to clear things up in the bridge club, but she was never sure who believed her. I decided then that adults were nosey and liked to make a big deal out of nothing.

S I X T E E N

I got a bad sore throat in October and was forced to stay home. My parents wondered if I was faking it, knowing I detested school, but it turned out to be my tonsils. I didn't mind. The doctor told me about the post-operation diet. No more orange juice, cod liver oil, oatmeal, or tomato soup. Just ice cream. Three meals a day plus a snack. I was suckered in. After the operation I was so sick I couldn't even think of ice cream. A few days later, Clancy dropped by with a foot-high stack of comic books. I couldn't read everything, but I looked at the pictures and understood enough to know what was going on.

Mary Lou even tried to be nice. She didn't always succeed, but I realized it wasn't natural. One evening after I started to feel better, Mary Lou and I were home alone waiting for my mother to return from grocery shopping. A fierce thunderstorm was in progress, and Mary Lou was under the dining room table, hands cupped over her ears, scared out of her wits.

"I can't stand it!" she screamed.

"We're safe in the house!" I shouted back.

121

Mary Lou continued to work herself into a frenzy. I tried to keep calm, but watching her was unsettling. It wasn't long before I joined her under the table.

"Who can we call?" she shouted, still holding her ears.

"I don't know," I said.

"We need help!"

"They'll just laugh at us."

"Who cares?" she cried. Her eyes were pleading. "I'm going to call Mrs. Bean."

"What can she do?"

Mary Lou looked hard at me, then crawled out from under the table. "She's next door."

She walked to the bay window and picked up the phone. The window projected out into the side yard and was only a short distance away from the Beans' bay window. A perfect place to spy on Mrs. Bean when there was nothing better to do. Mary Lou spent a lot of time there.

"Turn off the light," she said. She waited for the operator. "I don't want her to see us." She gave the number to the operator and waited.

I stood next to her and pressed my nose against the cool, wet glass. "I don't think she's home."

The Beans' house was dark, but I could see the phone across the way when lightning lit up the sky. I even heard their phone ring. "I guess not," said Mary Lou. She was calmer now that she was doing something.

Suddenly I saw a light. Someone opened a door. The

bathroom door. The Beans' dining room filled with light. "Look, Mary Lou. She's coming out of the bathroom."

"Oh my gosh!" shrieked Mary Lou. "She's naked!"

I started to giggle.

Mrs. Bean waddled through the dining room, her bulges throbbing like Jell-O. She reached for the phone.

"Hello, Mrs. Bean." Mary Lou motioned for me to come closer and listen.

"Who's this?" said Mrs. Bean. She tried wrapping a towel around her waist, but it didn't reach. She placed the towel on her hip and let it hang.

"It's me," said Mary Lou. "You know, Mary Lou next door." She pressed her hand against the receiver and tried to choke down the laughter. I thought she was going to explode.

"And what can I do for you, Dearie," said Mrs. Bean. She always said "dearie" to put us in our place.

Lightning flashed, and for a split second our dining room was as bright as noon. She saw us.

"Oh my God!" she screamed, then threw down the phone and ran. The crash of thunder was deafening. We observed the exit of the giant, pink elephant. When she reached the bathroom, she slammed the door, and suddenly we were staring into blackness.

Mary Lou giggled, then laughed, and finally clapped her hands and skipped around the table. I followed and around we went until we fell to our knees and pounded the floor with our fists. The lightning and thunder were forgotten. We sat against the wall and went over it again and again, laughing, then stopping when we were breathless. We were still on the floor when Mother walked in, loaded with groceries.

"Everything all right?" she shouted. She placed the sacks on the counter.

"Fine," said Mary Lou, then burst out laughing.

"What's so funny?"

"Nothing," said Mary Lou, but I knew she couldn't keep it a secret.

Mother was horrified when she heard what had happened. She made us promise never to tell anyone. That evening Mary Lou called Dunster and told her everything. I told Digger and Clancy when they came to visit the following day. Digger wanted to hear all the details, then made me repeat them again. Too bad he wasn't there. It would have meant a lot to him.

Mrs. Bean never realized how much she helped that night, and we never had the chance to tell her since she gave us the silent treatment. When I told Digger about it, he doubled Blackie's visits. A balancing of justice was always in progress.

I was still at home recuperating when Ernie came to our door one morning. He asked for work in exchange for a meal. He wore his golf knickers and cap, but since it was colder, he also wore an old, torn mackinaw. Men often came to the door and my mother never turned them down. She told Ernie to rake the leaves, a job my father didn't like, and one he'd postponed for over a month. Ernie worked hard for several hours and finished just before noon.

"Anything more?" he asked when Mother answered the door. She stepped outside to check out what he'd done, and for a moment I thought he recognized me.

Mother warmed up the leftovers from a roast and cooked a lot of potatoes and carrots. She invited him in and had him sit at the kitchen table. We watched as Ernie ate enough for ten men. I sat down across from him, resting my chin in my hands. He smelled like the out of doors. Mother ran next door to borrow some coffee.

"I know you," I said.

He looked up. "I thought I'd seen you before." He smiled.

"Your name is Ernie," I said.

"How did you know?"

"I'm Clancy's friend. We came to visit you last summer."

"I see," he said. The smile left his face. "Don't ever go there again."

"I know," I said, then sat up. "Do you live in those huts all winter?"

He took a piece of bread and soaked up all the gravy on his plate. "Yep," he said.

"Isn't it cold?"

"Not bad till it gets down around zero."

"What do you do then?"

"Just hibernate like a bear and wait for spring." He chuckled. "Some guys go down to Florida for the winter, but they lose their place when they come back."

"Do you work for the Turk?" I said.

He frowned. "Not exactly."

I heard Mother coming back. It was too bad. I had a lot more questions about the Turk. I stood up. "Don't tell her I know you," I said.

"Don't worry." He smiled again. "Cross my heart." He crossed himself just as Mother came in, and she looked surprised.

Ernie finished off with three pieces of pie and I don't know how many cups of coffee. Mother and I stood at the window and watched him walk across the back yard and head down the alley. "Those men sure eat a lot," she said. She shook her head and chuckled. "But I'm glad he was religious."

"How do you know?"

"He crossed himself," she said. "But it was different. Must be Greek Orthodox." I didn't say anything, but I told Clancy about it when he brought me a new stack of comic books.

"Why didn't you ask Ernie how he knew the Turk?" said Clancy.

"I didn't have time."

"Maybe Ernie works for the Turk?"

"Then why would the Turk go to the hobo village?"

"We've got to find out," said Clancy.

When I finally returned to school, I was shocked at

how much everyone had learned. Old Grizzly Bear had them stand up and read on and on about Dick and Jane and Spot, two dull children and their dog who was smarter than both of them put together. Dick and Jane spent most of their time smiling at the postman while Spot barked and wagged his tail. It was enough to make you sick. I could tell what was going on by the pictures even though I only understood half the words. Comic books were a lot more interesting. The characters had a lot more to do than stand around and grin. I thought I would never learn to read.

Everyone was all caught up with numbers. The teacher was set on proving that two and two equaled four, which seemed silly. Even I knew that. It was common knowledge in the neighborhood. I couldn't understand why anyone had to prove it when we were willing to take someone's word for it.

Mary Lou tried to help. She was embarrassed having a stupid little brother. Even Clancy tried, but it was no use. He couldn't begin to understand what it was like being ordinary. Old Grizzly Bear enjoyed making me stand and read just to listen to me struggle. It made her day. The time off had not been worth it. I knew that school was going to be even worse, if that was possible.

S E V E N T E E N

A Thanksgiving pageant was the kind of thing you could expect from old Grizzly Bear. Of course, we couldn't have done anything interesting with pilgrims and Indians. We had to be vegetables and fruits. Grizzly Bear made sure she never got behind anything that was fun. And talk about unfair. Some people got to be potatoes, apples, and pears. I was to be a pumpkin. But it could have been worse. Asparagus was rejected outright. I pleaded for something more respectable, but Grizzly Bear said it was already decided. I was given Penny Kristapoulis as my partner. She was a skinny little girl who wore thick glasses. Penny was to be a string bean, and we were to hold hands and walk down the aisle to the auditorium stage.

A pumpkin and a string bean with glasses. What could have been worse? I had nightmares about it, but none equalled the night of the performance. We were in the classroom getting ready to go on and five or six mothers were helping with costumes and putting on makeup. About ten minutes to go, they went crazy. Old Grizzly Bear shouted directions, but no one paid attention. Wally Bentz's mother got hysterical and old Grizzly Bear made her sit down and put her head between her legs.

We had to wear our Sunday best, which meant knickers, coat, and tie for boys. The costumes were made of stiff wire covered with colored cloth, and, with the coat underneath, I overheated. I could scarcely breath. I sat down behind the easel displaying a map of the world, and that's where Grizzly Bear spotted me. She rushed over and, without permission, painted my face to look like the stem of a pumpkin.

"That looks pretty good," she said, then stepped back, squinting her beady eyes. "Yes, you look fine." She nodded, took out a handkerchief, wet it with her tongue, and touched up my cheek. "Just right," she said.

I knew I was going to die from some terrible disease. Right there on the spot. I wanted to rub off the germs, but I was wired in too tight. I looked around at the noisy confusion and wanted to run, but the front and rear doors were locked. I had to hand it to old Grizzly Bear, she didn't miss a trick.

Someone called for us to find our partners. I spotted Penny surrounded by two mothers who were still fixing her costume. They had to cut bigger eye-holes for her glasses. When they finished, she looked ridiculous, nothing like a string bean. But then I hardly looked like a pumpkin.

Everyone lined up with their partner, and we

walked out into the hall and waited. I thought about running for it again, but it was too late. Wally Bentz's mother started playing *America the Beautiful* on the piano while we walked quickly to the auditorium door, then headed down the aisle toward the stage. Pairs of carrots, potatoes, apples, and peas, tomatoes, peaches, turnips, and clusters of grapes. Finally, at the very end, a pumpkin and a string bean. As Penny and I passed, people on both sides of the aisle pointed and snickered. Of course we looked stupid. What did they expect?

When we arrived at the steps to the stage, Penny tripped and crashed into me. Together we fell to the floor, wires bending, cloth ripping. Loud laughter followed.

I stood up. My costume was bent and torn. I looked at Penny. Her costume was half off, and her glasses hung from a bent wire. She started to cry.

I helped her straighten out her glasses, then we crawled up the stairs and hid behind the other fruits and vegetables. When they started to sing, Penny stopped crying, but neither of us opened our mouth. I felt like a fool.

Our class sang three songs, then the pageant ended with a violin solo by Wally Bentz. Mrs. Bentz knew he was a child prodigy and worked every angle to get him on the program. Maybe he was pretty good, but you could have fooled me.

Wally always played *Londonderry Aire.* For

Halloween, Thanksgiving, Christmas, and Washington's Birthday. I was sick of it.

But this performance turned out to be his best. He was dressed like a turnip, and when a wire from his costume broke loose and tore the violin strings, a loud cheer came from the stage. Mrs. Bentz, accompanying Wally on the piano, was beside herself. Mr. Bentz ran forward and started fixing the instrument, while old Grizzly Bear stepped forward and told several jokes. No one laughed. When she announced the violin was fixed and the solo was about to resume, a moan came from the stage. The audience clapped politely.

Afterward, at the table where red punch and cookies were served, my father and mother told Mrs. Bentz Wally's performance was good. I knew I'd hear about it later. Wally stood behind his mother, close to the table. He looked both ways, then stuffed his pockets full of cookies. Maybe there was hope for old Wally after all.

Roosevelt was elected for a second term. My father figured we were on the road to hell. Digger's grandfather celebrated for weeks. He even found a job, but it lasted only a few months. Of all the families in the neighborhood, they seemed to have it the roughest. But they never complained.

Rudy's family got along pretty well, even though five children at Catholic school must have strained a fireman's wages. They were good Democrats and during the campaign they had a large poster of Roosevelt in their living room window. Rudy's father celebrated the victory, then came home and gave all the kids a crewcut. Unfortunately Rudy was included. Her mother refused to let her attend her brother Mike's first communion. It was that bad.

Rudy didn't care one way or the other, but she said her mother went nuts and tore the kitchen cabinets off the wall. It got her father's attention.

My father couldn't understand how Clancy's dad, a lawyer—or anyone with an education—could be a Democrat. Most everyone else in the neighborhood were Republicans. My father could go for an afternoon stroll and talk politics with almost anyone who came along.

While Rudy's mother was upset about the crewcut, we thought it best to stay away from her place. We tried out Clancy's clothes chute and it turned out better than we expected. It was two stories high and narrow, but the fall was spectacular. Unfortunately, Bernie Heifitz got stuck between the first and second floor and Grumble's dad had to come to pry him out. Bernie had this knack for messing up a good thing. We were forbidden to use the chute after that, and we never did unless Clancy's mother was away.

E I G H T E E N

When cold weather arrived, Clancy and I were surprised. We both had the same leather coat and hat our mothers bought the year before from Marshall Fields. The coat had a fur collar, a copy of the one Charles Lindberg wore. The coat was already too small, yet too expensive to discard. It was like a strait jacket, but the hat was even worse. It took both hands and all my mother's weight to force the hat on. It was so tight. I couldn't smile. Clancy finally refused to wear his hat and so did I. Miraculously my headaches went away.

On school days Clancy stayed for lunch, but Digger and I always met and walked home together. We ran, jumped fences, waded mud puddles, and picked a different way every time. When snow fell, we threw snowballs at cars, the patrolman at the crossing, barking dogs, and anything that moved.

One day we passed the reflecting pond in Becker's back yard. It wasn't very big or deep, but it had just frozen and had to be tested. Digger insisted on going first and who was I to argue? One step, and the ice cracked.

"Guess we better wait," I said.

"Try it?" said Digger. "You don't weigh as much."

"I'm not crazy."

"I know," he said. "You're scared." His chin went out, and I wanted to knock it off.

"You're like my sister," I said. "I've been suckered in before."

"If you're scared, just say so." Digger put his hands on his hips.

I looked at the ice. I knew it was going to be a disaster. But what else could I do? "All right," I said.

I took the first step, held my breath, then took a second. CRACK! The ice parted and I dropped into hip-deep water. It was so cold it hurt.

Digger put out his arm, grinning. I pulled myself out without his help.

"Are you all right?" he said, still gloating.

"What does it look like?" I stood there shivering.

"I tried it too, you know."

"Hah! That's a good one."

"All right, be a sorehead."

I reached down and tried to wring water out of my knickers, then turned and headed for home. Digger followed, but I refused to talk. All I could think about was how I was going to catch it.

I slipped up the back steps and tiptoed into the kitchen. No one there. It was Monday. My mother was still downstairs turning out the weekly wash.

A wild idea hit me. I took off my wet shoes, socks,

and knickers, then placed them in the oven. The hope was to bake them dry before my mother came upstairs. It had to work. I turned on the gas, then went in search of matches. A bad idea. When I returned and lit the match, there was a blinding flash! Then the explosion! I staggered back, covered my face, and fell into a chair. I was stunned, yet felt no pain. And I wasn't blinded. But there was a strange smell. Burned hair.

My mother burst into the kitchen. "What happened?" she screamed. She touched my forehead. "Are you all right?" She stepped back for a better look. "You don't have any eyebrows!" She burst out laughing and dropped into a chair. "Or eyelashes!" More laughter. "And no hair in front."

She wiped her eyes and drew me in. "I'm glad you're not hurt." She hugged me, then insisted I stay home for the rest of the day. It took three months before I had eyebrows and lashes again.

We always passed the Turk's back yard on the way home after school. It was right across the alley from Becker's. We rarely saw the Turk, but a couple of his ugly cats were always wandering around. It was hard to say how many cats he had. There always seemed to be a different one.

If it hadn't been for Digger's grandfather, we wouldn't have given the Turk so much attention. He told Digger that people from Turkey were Moslem and that they had harems. That caught Clancy's attention. He started reading up on it. He said that Moslems prayed five times a day on their knees, facing east. And they prayed to Allah. We were dying to see him do it because Clancy said that Moslems always wore a sword with a wide curving blade when they prayed. And if anyone saw them, they were obliged by holy law to cut their head off. We spent hours spying, but he never did much of anything except feed the cats.

My father knew him well enough to call him by his first name, which I could never pronounce. He said the Turk was a good man, but he allowed young boys to play in his pool hall which was against the law. My father dropped in every so often to remind him. Thanksgiving weekend I went along on one of his visits, and even though my father told him off, the Turk gave me a Baby Ruth bar. He seemed to listen to what my father said. I sensed that the Turk liked him.

There was also the question of why the Turk visited Ernie at the hobo village—they had been talking like old friends. It didn't make sense.

Several weeks before Christmas, Digger and I were playing last tag on our way home for lunch. He chased me down the alley, and I spotted the Turk through a crack in his fence. I stopped, and Digger plowed into me, knocking us both to the ground. I knew he did it on purpose.

"What the hell, Digger!" I said. He grinned and rolled off. "Didn't you see him?" I nodded toward the fence.

"The Turk?" he said. His eyes angled up and he

turned slowly. "Let's check him out."

I got to the knothole first, and Digger had to be satisfied with the space between the boards. We hunkered down to our favorite pastime.

The Turk was in shirt sleeves, which was surprising. A wind off the lake was cold. He was partially hidden by a bush and it was hard to see what he was doing.

"I think he's digging a hole," I whispered.

"What for?" Digger said.

The Turk pulled an old paint can out of the ground and brushed off the dirt. Red paint was streaked down one side, and rust and dirt made it appear like it had been buried for a long time. He studied the contents, then looked around. Finally he walked to the back door and followed one of his cats inside.

"What was that all about?" said Digger.

"I don't know," I said. "What was in the can?"

Digger's eyes glistened. "Gold," he said.

"No, really?"

"I don't know. But he acts like it's important."

"Let's come back later," I said.

After school we grabbed Clancy and made sure we avoided Bernie. Bernie would have fouled it up. But Clancy was excited.

On the way home we talked about what was in the can. Digger figured it was precious jewels, Clancy said it was filled with the ashes of a dead wife from his harem, and I said it held a secret invention for spying on America. After that, the ideas got too ridiculous. When we arrived at the Turk's fence, we dropped to our knees and crawled the last few feet. Digger and I fought over the knothole. Clancy took the space between the boards, and I joined him there. This was no time for a fight with Digger.

"See anything?" whispered Clancy.

"Over there," whispered Digger. "Where the cat's scratching around." He stood and threw a stone over the fence, then dropped down again. The rock landed close, and the cat sniffed it before strutting off.

"Looks like someone's covered up the hole," I said.

"Maybe he buried it again?" said Digger. No one spoke for awhile. "Shall we do it?" said Digger.

"What?" I said. I knew what he meant, but I didn't want to even think about it.

"Dig it up," said Digger.

"Quiet," I whispered. "Want him to hear us?"

"He's at work," said Digger. "He's never here."

"Like today when we saw him?"

"Come on, you guys," said Clancy. "Let's just do it?"

"We could wait until dark," I said. I was thinking of the sword with the curving blade.

"Now," said Digger. He snickered. "We'll dig it up, put a note in it, then bury it again."

"Great," said Clancy. "He'll wonder who did it."

"What will the note say?" I said.

"Let's dig it up and then decide," said Clancy.

"Who's got a pencil and paper?" I said. Clancy never

was good on detail.

"Shit," said Digger. He stood up and looked around.

"You're closer to home," said Clancy.

"What do you mean?" I said. "It's the same for both of us."

"Jeez," said Digger. "Are you going to screw it up?" He glared at me.

"All right," I said. I ran home and returned with pencil and paper. Digger and Clancy were already inside the back yard, opening the can. I was mad they couldn't wait. "What is it?" I shouted.

"Shut up," said Clancy with his chin out. He looked like a bulldog.

"Looks like a bunch of papers," said Digger.

"And money!" said Clancy, as he lifted the papers and looked underneath.

"A lot of money," I said. Clancy held up two large rolls of bills held together by a rubber band.

"How much?" said Digger, pushing me aside for a closer look.

"Probably a million," said Clancy.

"Could even be a thousand," said Digger. He wiped his nose with his wrist.

"We're rich," I said.

Clancy spun around. "What are you talking about?"

"It's buried treasure, isn't it?"

"Sure," said Clancy. "And it belongs to the Turk." We looked at each other.

"So what shall we do?" I said.

"Write a note," said Digger. "Didn't we agree?"

"What'll we say?" said Clancy.

"Let's sign our names," I said. It was the only thing I could write decently.

"Are you crazy?" said Clancy. "Do you want the police on us?"

"No," I said.

"Let's write a big 'Z' for Zorro," said Digger. He looked around for approval.

Clancy's face slid into a grin. "Yeah, that's good," he said.

"So who's gonna do it?" I said.

"You've got the pencil and paper," said Clancy.

"I'll screw it up," I said. I usually wrote Z backwards.

"Geez," said Clancy. He grabbed the pencil and paper and scrawled out a large Z, then placed the paper face up in the can, put on the lid, and dropped it into the hole. We all helped cover it with dirt.

That's all we talked about the rest of the week, but when we returned a week later, we couldn't find it. The Turk had moved it. But where? We searched around until dark but couldn't find a trace of new digging.

"Guess he hid it somewhere else," said Clancy. He looked disappointed.

"Yeah," said Digger. "And it was a thousand dollars."

"A million," said Clancy. I nodded agreement with Clancy. Digger smacked me on the arm.

Several weeks later, during a guilty moment, I confessed everything to my father. At first he was upset, but when he calmed down he told me the Turk was like a lot of people who didn't trust the banks and kept his money and valuables hidden.

"Do you know where the can is now?" said my father.

"No," I said. "But it's not in the back yard. It couldn't be. We spent hours looking."

"Good," said my father. "Now don't go there again. Ever. Understand?"

I nodded.

N I N E T E E N

Christmas vacation was just a few days away. Two weeks out of school and away from old Grizzly Bear was too good to be true. We struggled to make it through without a problem, and there were only a few slip-ups. Like too many boos after Wally Bentz's violin solo at the Christmas Assembly, and Grizzly Bear got nailed with a snowball at recess. It was never proven who did it, although everyone was sure it was Maxie Grover. He was good to have around to take most of the heat.

Maxie was a fighter. He carved his initials in the desk top, removed the screws from the desk until it collapsed, and dipped Carol Simkins's pigtails in the inkwell. On special days he broke windows, set the waste basket on fire, or triggered the fire alarm.

The principal, Miss Wolfe, was even older and slower than old Grizzly Bear. And she was out to tame Maxie if it killed her. At least twice a week she'd waddle in, snatch Maxie by the ear, and drag him out screaming. Maxie put on a real show digging in his heels. Afterward he'd report what had happened. Miss

Wolfe would bend him over a chair in her office and let him have it with a wooden paddle. But the harder she whacked, the louder he laughed. We could hear it echoing through the cold air return. He loved it.

"No nerves in his ass," said Clancy.

Maxie was a kind of symbol for freedom. He didn't do it to gain praise or attention. He was a natural revolutionary.

Friday afternoon Clancy and I walked past the principal's office and found the door was open a crack. We could see Maxie in there taking his licks, but, instead of laughing, he was acting bored. A new strategy to drive Miss Wolfe crazy. We wondered which one would win.

On the way home we saw Dunster, who never said hello because we were Digger's friends. Dunster was a good student and so busy with homework she hadn't nailed Digger in weeks. Digger was growing careless. He went wherever he pleased, stopped looking over his shoulder, and didn't check out the trees. It was a mistake. The first day of Christmas vacation Dunster was waiting for him on Clancy's garage roof and dropped on him as he came through the back gate.

Clancy and I were on the back porch when we heard the scream. We ran over and found him lying on his back with a small, metal sand bucket, the kind we took to the beach, stuck to his tongue. Warm, wet flesh sticking to cold, dry metal.

"What happened?" said Clancy. Digger rolled his

eyes back and forth.

"Let's take him inside," I said.

We pulled Digger up and walked him into Clancy's kitchen, the bucket still attached. His mother applied hot towels and soon Digger was freed.

"How'd she get at your tongue?" said Clancy.

Digger glared. "How should I know?"

"I thought since you were there . . ."

"None of your business," said Digger. There were tears in his eyes.

I still didn't buy Bernie's attitude toward Christmas and spent a lot of time checking out his house and yard. I knew I'd spot an ornament, some mistletoe, something. I was disappointed. Then one evening a bunch of candles appeared in the living room window. Proof at last. Old Bernie was faking all along. I raced home to report it to my father, but he explained that it was a Hanukkah icon, an ancient tradition that had nothing to do with Christmas. I was depressed.

Christmas morning, as I opened presents in front of the tree, I couldn't help thinking of Bernie. What value was there in being different from everyone else? Particularly about Christmas. Bernie wasn't easy to like, but I had to respect him.

I also had lost faith in Santa Claus. There was no snow on Christmas Eve, and Christmas Day, after all the excitement of new toys was over, I asked my father about a sleigh landing and taking off from a roof that was rough as sandpaper. He shrugged and said there were a lot of things we didn't understand. The whole thing made me wonder about Jesus. Adults had a way of setting you up. It was the same answer I got in Sunday school when I asked about life after death. The idea made me uncomfortable. Eternity sounded frightening, like a long, lonely journey into nothing.

When snow fell the day after Christmas, we built walls and igloos under the monkey tree and spent hours defending our fortress. Grand battles took place with walls destroyed and rebuilt between attacks. Sometimes we'd stop the battle to pepper a car with snowballs. Each time the black Packard went by, we let go with a barrage. The driver never stopped, and the other men looked straight ahead, like we didn't exist. We tried harder the next time they passed. It was cold, wet, wonderful. I wanted Christmas vacation to last forever. New Year's Day the sun came out and by late afternoon the snow was gone. It was depressing.

The last day of vacation was cold and overcast. We stood in mud at the base of the largest tree and looked at what was left of yesterday's snow forts. The tree house was still wet, and the cables were too cold to enjoy. "We've got to do something important," said Clancy.

"Like what?" said Digger. He was in a lousy mood because Dunster had caught him and thrown him in Becker's reflecting pool. He had to go home for dry clothes and made us all wait, so we weren't in a good mood either.

"Let's go to the hobo village," said Clancy.

"Ernie doesn't want us around," I said.

"He doesn't have to see us," said Clancy.

"What about Rudy?" I said. She was wearing her brother Mike's old coat and a wool cap that practically covered her face.

"No one would guess she's a girl," said Clancy.

"There's nothing to do around here," said Digger.

We headed out, and when we passed the gangster's house, Digger threw a snowball at the front window. The snowball left a nice, white scar on the brick. We all joined in and soon the house was covered with spots. We would have continued, but the driver of the black Packard stepped out on the porch and we ran across the highway.

We kept up a running battle until we reached the tracks. The boxcars still had snow on the tops, and dirty snow hid much of the gravel. We crossed several empty tracks, then crawled under two lines of cars. It was easier than in summer, but our knickers got soaked. The tracks were empty now and we could see the hobo village.

Clancy looked around. My hands and wet knees were freezing, and Rudy looked like she was suffering. Clancy turned and started up the ladder of a boxcar. The rest of us grumbled. When we reached the top, the snow made every step perilous. Rudy slipped once and was caught by Digger.

"Look at that," said Clancy. He pointed toward the

village. Smoke from fires in most of the huts spiraled upward, and two men sat on a log in front of an open fire. A gray, smokey haze hung low over the roofs, and the ground was a sea of mud.

"Doesn't look too nice," I said.

"It looks horrible," said Rudy. "Let's go."

"Wait a minute," said Clancy. He was squinting.

Then I noticed the Turk's car pull up and stop. Ernie and the Turk got out, loaded up with boxes of groceries, and headed for the open fire. The two men stood and shouted, and suddenly more men appeared. "Interesting," said Digger.

Ernie and the Turk passed out loaves of bread and sacks of flower, then Ernie and two others walked back to the car and loaded up. The Turk stayed and talked. Ernie passed out the remaining food, then headed back to the car with the Turk. By the time the Turk drove off, most of the men had returned to their huts and the place looked empty.

"Can you believe that?" said Clancy.

"Do you think the Turk feeds all those guys?" said Rudy.

"Looks like it," said Clancy.

"I wonder why?" said Digger.

"Because he's a nice guy," said Rudy. Her teeth were chattering. "Now can we go?"

"Maybe that's how he spends all his money," said Clancy. He grabbed my arm. "Here comes a brakeman."

We ran for the ladder, and this time I slipped off half way down and I landed on my back in wet snow. Digger pulled me up. We crawled under the next line of cars and ran. There wasn't time to be scared.

School began again, relieved only by lemon drops during the long afternoons while Old Grizz droned on about Dick, Jane, and Spot. She had water on the brain.

Word got out that she planned to hold me back to repeat the second grade. It couldn't be true. But when I accidently overheard my parents talking, I knew I was in trouble. My father thought I wasn't out with tonsillitis long enough to fall that far behind. My mother didn't know what to think. I was grateful he never mentioned it. I guess they hoped for a miracle. I know I did.

The dark days of winter passed slowly with nothing to separate one day from the other except for the time Carol Simkins, the teacher's pet, didn't make it to the rest room. She didn't even make it out of her seat. One late February morning Old Grizz turned her ankle during a fire drill. Both events were celebrated out on the playground.

Twice in February the school nurse came and made us line up for an inoculation. She was pretty in her white uniform, and she smiled a lot, but after the first needle no one trusted her. She was part of the system. And all the screaming got on your nerves. Teddy

Billows, the biggest and fattest kid in the class, passed out. But why not? School was a place they beat up children and stuck them with needles. What else could I expect?

T W E N T Y

Wally Bentz gave us a little excitement one cloudy afternoon. It happened right after recess, and Old Grizz was reading us a story about some Dutch kid who stuck his finger in the dike and saved all of Holland. I didn't believe it for a minute, but she had to dramatize it, dancing around with her spit flying. She used a high voice for women and a low voice for men. She thought she was wonderful. The only one listening was Carol Simkins, who sat on the front row smiling. That's how you made it big in school.

Old Grizz was just finishing the story when Wally shot out of his seat like a stone from a slingshot. His eyes were bugged out, his face was maggot white, and he just stared at Old Grizz to let her know he was in trouble. He started for the back door while she watched in horror. After a hundred years in the classroom, she knew what to expect. Wally reached for the door knob, dropped to his knees, retched once, twice, then threw up all over the door. It looked like an orange-speckled coat of paint.

There were screams, groans. And we all stood up

and backed away. Wally shook his head, looked around, then slowly dragged himself to his feet and headed for the front door. He attempted a smile, but suddenly his eyes rolled up and his face switched back to panic. He lurched forward, his legs stiff, his back arched.

Come on Wally—we know you can make it. But even before he reached for the knob he dropped to his knees, threw up again, and covered the front door. This time it was purple. Old Wally must have been storing it up for a week.

I looked at Grover, then Clancy. We were trapped like rats in a wash tub. Carol Simkins screamed, Old Grizz just stood there open-mouthed, and Teddy Billows passed out, hitting his desk top with a thump. Clancy and Maxie grabbed a chair, crawled up, and threw open a window. Our school was single story and it wasn't far to the ground. Maxie was halfway out the window before Old Grizz grabbed him and practically yanked his pants off pulling him in. During the action, her knee-length underwear showed, which was enough to make you sick.

"Calm down!" she yelled. "Everyone!" But the air was so bad she finally cracked and screamed for the janitor. Maxie ran to the front of the room, grabbed the mallet, and broke the glass on the fire alarm.

We all crawled up on our desk tops and watched the other classes parade out on the playground into six inches of new snow. When Old Grizz spotted the principal, she screamed out the open window. "We're trapped!"

Miss Wolfe waddled back through the snow. "What are you doing in there?" she shouted.

"We can't get out!" shrieked Old Grizz.

"What's wrong?" Miss Wolfe stood on her toes and tried to peer in the window.

"There isn't time. Just get the janitor."

"You're sure?"

"Hurry!" yelled Old Grizz. Of course, "hurry" was not a possibility. It was a long time before the janitor finally arrived. He flung the door open, then jumped back. It must have looked pretty bad up close. He had to run back to the boiler room for his equipment. And when he returned, he threw sand all over the place. Old Grizz was the first one out the door, and she ran down the hall, which was something to see. When she returned from the principal's office, we were all in the hall taking deep breaths. She told us we were released for the rest of the day. Everyone cheered until she warned us that we'd have to stay if we couldn't leave quietly. Instantly there was silence. Poor Wally was still slumped in his desk as we walked out.

After that, we included Wally at recess and found out he was pretty normal. We questioned him about what he'd eaten, since the orange and purple had us all guessing. We had high hopes of taking turns doing the same thing. But Wally had no idea what it was. Several days later Maxie experimented with pickles and milk.

He wasn't able to finish off one door let alone two. We told Wally that he was the best, and any time he wanted to try a repeat it was all right with us.

A month later during recess, Wally got a little careless and was hauled in for taking a leak in the bushes behind the auditorium. At that point he was truly one of the crowd since no respectable second grade boy ever used the rest room if he could help it. Unfortunately the shrubs were dying. Old Grizz took it upon herself to police the area every recess, which stopped us, but the neighborhood dogs took over and finished them off.

When brown winter grass turned green and fruit trees came into blossom and the days grew warm and long, I was so filled with hope that I couldn't stand it. For no reason I would suddenly laugh out loud or smack Maxie on the back of the head, even throw a spit ball at Clancy across the room. I knew it was only a matter of time. They had to let us out.

Poor Maxie was beside himself. He was in the principal's office every other day, laughing away while Miss Wolfe whacked him with a paddle. Maxie had returned to laughing, the bored look hadn't worked. Miss Wolfe was a maniac. And Maxie was amazing. About three every afternoon, he'd try to see how long he could hold his breath, his way of making it through the last half hour in class. He'd sit up, take a deep breath, then hold it and watch the clock, his lips sucked in, his face slowly turning blue. Some days it got to be frightening, as the second hand approached one minute. Clancy said that oxygen debt could cause brain damage. I wasn't sure what that meant, but it sounded like it had already happened to Maxie.

All eyes were on him every time he held and counted, except for Simkins. She maintained her endless grin, as Old Grizz went on and on with one of her favorite stories. But we were always quiet. It was the easiest period of the day.

The first week in April, Maxie set the record of forty-eight seconds. He also turned blue, passed out, fell out of his desk, and hit the floor like a sack of sand. For a moment, we thought he was a goner, but he woke up.

It was the kind of thing you could expect where depression and boredom were common. Maybe Miss Griswald and Miss Wolfe had another side, but I never saw it. For Maxie and me, along with most of the boys, school was a world of grouchy old women who didn't begin to understand.

By mid-May, each day gave us reason to be more hopeful. The day for the school picnic a soft rain fell and the picnic was postponed. Picnics and field trips were always scheduled for rainy days. That was the most important lesson I learned in school.

Clancy found a mouse on the way to school one morning. It was cold and wet, so he dried it off and put it in his pocket. Once in the classroom he showed everyone his new pet. "Let me see him," whispered Maxie, and immediately he had the frightened creature in his hand. Class was in session, and Grizz was at the blackboard copying addition problems, organizing the day's torture.

"It's my turn," I whispered, and pushed Wally Bentz's hand away. Wally pushed back and a silent battle started. But I kept my eye on Grizz. After some hard talking, Maxie let me have the mouse. It was warm in the palm of my hand. I settled back, enjoying the mouse, when an idea popped into my head.

"Can I let it go?" I asked Clancy.

"No!" he said, louder than he should have. Grizz spun around, but we were now too skilled to be caught easily. Everything looked normal. Grizz returned to the blackboard, and I told Clancy what I had in mind. The plan was to reach around and slip the mouse under Simkins's skirt. By spring, Simkins had become a target. She sat in front of me, placed there to settle down an unruly area.

Clancy thought about it. "Okay," he whispered. I checked Grizz one more time. She was making a list of three-letter words for a spelling test.

I looked back at Clancy. "Now?" He nodded.

I reached down under Simkins's desk and hit my elbow. It felt like an electric shock. My hand flew open, and the mouse ended up in her lap. She leaped out of her seat, screaming. The mouse flew across the aisle and landed in Penny Kristapoulis's hair. She screamed, jumped up, and her glasses flew across the room.

Grizz spun around, then waddled down the aisle and grabbed me. "What's going on?" she shouted.

"Nothing," I said. The moist, sour cloud surrounded me. Grizz looked across the room at the girls popping out of their seats like jumping jacks. It was clear where the mouse was headed.

"Then what's all the fuss?" she said.

"There's a mouse," screamed Simkins. She started to cry. Grizz drew her in and held her.

"That's all right," said Grizz in a soft, comforting tone.

Clancy gave me an elbow, then pointed to the floor. Grizz and Simkins were standing in a growing puddle of water. I choked back the laughter until I looked at Clancy, and we both let go. By then everyone but Grizz knew what had happened. Simkins was never that dependable under normal conditions—excited, she was totally unreliable. Grizz finally looked down, gasped, then stepped back.

We took an early recess, and once out on the playground Maxie let the mouse go. We watched the little guy flee. Maxie said that Simkins was a kind of symbol. When she buckled we had every right to question the entire system.

By early afternoon I was sure Simkins had squealed. Her confident smirk confirmed it. Just before the final bell, Grizz leaned across my desk as the cloud descended. "I'd like to see you after school," she said.

I knew I was in for it. "Yes, ma'am," I said, then

watched Maxie Grover, growing bluer by the second, trying to set a new record. I soon forgot what she said. Maxie didn't reach forty-five seconds before he passed out, but this time we had him propped up in his seat. It was tidier that way.

When the bell rang, I ran out and was halfway across the playground before I heard my name called. "Come back!" shouted Grizz.

I stopped and turned to see her hanging out the classroom window. "Shit," I said. The sun felt warm on my face, and I was desperate to leave. "So long," I said to Clancy. "The old bag wants to see me."

"Simkins?"

"I guess."

"Lots of luck," he said, then ran off. I watched him until he caught up with Digger.

Old Grizz was grading papers when I walked in, probably scribbling "FAIL" at the top of every sheet. She knew I was there.

"Yes, Miss Griswald," I said, finally. I wanted to get it over with.

"Sit down," she said without looking up. I slipped into the seat directly in front of her and slumped down so that I could barely see her. "Have any idea why I called you in?"

"No, ma'am," I said. I braced myself for the worst.

She looked up. "Certainly you must have some idea?"

"Not exactly," I said.

"It's about your schoolwork," she said.

That was close. "Yes, ma'am," I said.

She looked hard at me and her beady eyes drove in. "It's not very good, you know."

I nodded politely.

She looked at the clock, then dug into her purse and pulled out three orange pills. She chucked them one at a time and washed them down with a gulp of water. Normally she took them earlier in the day. We figured they were supposed to calm her down so she wouldn't kill Maxie.

"What do you think we should do about it?"

"About what?" I said. I was thinking about where Digger and Clancy would be.

"Your schoolwork."

What kind of a question was that? "We" never did anything. She did and we followed. That's the way it worked. "I don't know," I said.

"Well." She attempted a smile. "As much as I hate to do it, I'm going to have to hold you back."

"What do you mean?"

"Repeat the second grade," she said.

I sat up and looked down at the floor. The base of the desk had a black line of dirt where it met oak flooring. "I've already talked to your parents," she said.

I couldn't think. "My dad won't let you do that," I said.

"He's already agreed," she said.

I glared at her, hoping that she was wrong, yet

158

knowing that somehow she had succeeded. I didn't go home after school and arrived late for dinner. I asked my father if it was true, and he said that it was. He looked sad. I rushed past him, ran to my room, and missed dinner that evening. I cried myself to sleep.

TWENTY-ONE

School let out mid-morning on the last day. I raced home, changed into shorts and a polo shirt, then stepped out into a bright sun. School was behind me now. I was ready to proceed with the important things.

I went directly to the monkey tree, climbed to the platform, moved across the cables to the second tree, and swung to the third. Wind burned my eyes as I swung down to the ground. A ritual cleansing. I crawled back up to the platform and looked out across the park. I felt sure I'd see Digger and Clancy any moment. Rudy still had another few days of school. I thought we had it rough.

The black Packard pulled into the driveway across the street, then into the garage. Two men jumped out and took shotguns out of the back seat. The driver closed the door. I wondered what they were doing.

I was still thinking about them when Digger and Clancy walked under the tree. They were still in knickers. I couldn't believe it. "Come on you guys," I shouted, then took the cable to the ground. "You're late."

"It was Dunster," said Clancy. "You know." His eyes

moved to Digger.

Digger wouldn't look at me. I felt sorry for him. Dunster's attacks had increased since the weather got better. I wondered whether her need for raw violence would ever stop. Then there was Digger's dog. All Blackie did when Dunster beat up Digger was stand around and whine. A haymaker got no more than a snarl. The stupid dog actually liked Dunster.

The week before we found a sweater in the park that Clancy swore belonged to Dunster. We wrapped the sweater around a stick, then beat Blackie with it, hoping the combination of smell and pain might turn him against her. The next time Dunster showed up at the park, old Blackie couldn't get there fast enough to lick her hand. That made Clancy suspicious. The next day he spotted Dunster feeding Blackie a Butterfinger. How many it took, we never knew. Dunster was clever, you had to give her credit.

But school was out, and Digger had cheated death another day. We climbed up to the platform, laid back, and looked up into the new leaves.

"What do you think?" said Digger. "Another tunnel?"

"Why not," said Clancy.

"We should connect the other two," I said.

"Where's your shovel?" said Digger.

"I forgot it, but what are we waiting for?" I jumped up, grabbed a cable, swung down, then swung up again and dropped into a mound of last year's weeds and leaves. It was hard and needed to be replaced. There were so many things to be done. I jumped up and ran for home.

An important change was in progress. The joy of arboreal life was being replaced with a new fondness for burrowing. Classic evolution. Moving out of the trees onto the savannah.

The vacant lot across from the monkey tree was ideal—the lot we had burned the summer before. The growth had returned, and the black soil was soft, at least for the first few feet, and already there was a labyrinth of tunnels that drew kids from blocks away. All were built pretty much the same. First, a trench was dug. We had to dodge roots, so it was always crooked, although we couldn't keep a straight line if we tried. The trench was covered with old boards, sheet metal, and scraps of anything we could find. Then a foot of dirt was piled on top. The surface of the lot looked like a giant mole had gone berserk. And the dark, moist tunnels, filled with beetles, spiders, and mice, were cool, mysterious, perfect for hot afternoons. Unfortunately, cave-ins were frequent because of lousy workmanship. The week before, Digger's grandmother came looking for him and fell through the roof. We hauled her out and she laughed. I think she was embarrassed. No one was ever hurt except for Maxie's labrador who was in the tunnels when Maxie called. The dog crashed through the roof and cut his nose. Blackie was incapable of that kind of loyalty.

After a week of vacation, tunnels covered the entire lot. We crawled for hours in dark coolness, a candle the only light. That's when Bernie Heifitz dropped by. He always had to make sure it was something great before he got involved.

Digger and Clancy were placing boards on the roof, and Rudy and I were shoveling dirt on top. No one paid attention to Bernie.

"What are you guys doing?" said Bernie. He unwrapped a Baby Ruth bar.

"What does it look like?" said Clancy.

"Digging a tunnel," said Bernie.

"You guessed it," said Digger.

"He's a genius," mumbled Clancy.

Bernie was possibly as bright as Clancy, but he had to constantly demonstrate it. Clancy was apologetic about his intellect. Bernie used it like a weapon. But at times he could really be stupid.

"But why so deep?" said Bernie.

"Someone tell him," I said, then heaved another shovel full of dirt.

"Its going to be a clubhouse," said Digger.

"A clubhouse?" said Bernie. "Can I join?" Rudy and I stopped shoveling and Digger dropped the board he was putting in place.

"Sure," said Digger. He stood up straight and placed his hands on his hips. "You can if you're initiated."

"Initiated?" said Rudy. Her eyes popped out of her

blackened face.

"Of course," snapped Digger. He gave Rudy a warning glance. I looked down at the scar on my wrist.

"Okay," said Bernie. He took a bite from his candy bar. "What do I have to do?" His open mouth was swimming in chocolate and nuts.

"It's like this," said Digger. "We can't tell you now. Just come tomorrow. We'll have everything ready." He smiled. Clancy and Rudy cracked their dirty faces grinning.

"One more thing," said Digger. He talked out of the corner of his mouth. "Better pass around that Baby Ruth. Club members share everything." That just about killed old Bernie. Digger snatched it away and took a big bite. Bernie winced like it was part of his body. Clancy took a bite and Bernie recoiled again. I took a bite, then Rudy finished it off.

"Tomorrow," said Digger. Bernie stood there open-mouthed. "And don't forget a shovel." Digger stared him down.

"Yeah," said Bernie. "See you tomorrow." His voice cracked when he said "tomorrow."

As soon as Bernie was out of earshot, we dropped into the hole and laughed our guts out, pounding each other on the back. Rudy got the worst of it but didn't complain. We finally wore ourselves out and went back to work.

Bernie arrived with his shovel the next day and stood there waiting for us to say something. All morning we had praised Digger on how slick he'd talked Bernie into an initiation. Digger was all puffed up with himself. He let Bernie wait for some time before he stopped shoveling. "You ready?" he said.

"Yeah," said Bernie. He must have had tomato juice or spaghetti for lunch. A red ring surrounded his mouth.

"Okay," snapped Digger. "Take off your shirt."

"What for?" said Bernie.

"You'll see," said Clancy. He gave Bernie a push.

Bernie toyed with a button, then slowly removed his shirt. His skin was sheet-white and his blubber made a fold across his belly button.

"Okay," said Digger. "Down in the tunnel and on your back."

Bernie shook his head. "First tell me what you're going to do."

"Come on, Bernie," said Clancy. "We don't have time to explain."

Bernie's eyes jumped from Clancy, to Rudy, to Digger, to me. He waited. We stared. Finally he shrugged, dropped into the open trench, then crawled into the mouth of the tunnel and lay on his back. "That's better," said Digger. We could see him through the foot-square hole in the roof we'd made that morning for the ceremony.

Digger dropped to his knees and poked his head through the hole. "Move this way a little," he said. His voice echoed in the chamber. "Perfect," he said, then withdrew and brushed off his knees. "You guys ready?"

Of course we were ready. We had been since early morning. He motioned for us to gather with our candles. "Ready?" he said again. We nodded. "All right, let's begin." Digger struck a match, lit his candle, then lit the other candles. We stood motionless, waiting for the wax to melt. "When I say 'drip,'" he whispered, "let the wax fall."

"What was that?" shouted Bernie.

"Nothing!" shouted Digger. He looked at us. "Ready?"

"Yeah," said Rudy. Her voice faltered.

Digger studied the candle, his eyes reflecting the flame. We repeated the chant: "Great-green-gobs-of-greasy-grimy-gopher-guts."

"Drip!" shouted Digger. Wax was in the air.

Bernie screamed, went berserk, then lunged through the hole in the roof, and sent boards, dirt, and the four of us flying. He dove at Digger, tore his candle away, and threw it as hard as he could. I watched the candle disappear behind a garage roof. He forced the candles from the rest of us and threw them, then ran for home still whimpering.

I struggled to my feet. The others followed. No one spoke. Digger had done it again. He couldn't come up with a decent initiation to save his neck. We returned to our work grumbling.

In less than an hour, Bernie was back with his shovel. Without speaking, he started digging. Sometimes Bernie was hard to figure out. Maybe the wax hadn't hurt that much. We would never know. Another ceremony no one wanted to repeat.

T W E N T Y - T W O

Soon underground club houses were in progress all over the lot. Each one was larger than the last. A square shape would have made more sense since the roof planks were usually the same length. However, there was some primal need for a round shape, a kiva.

Digger insisted that we build the largest and deepest, which we did, and all the other kids were envious. It was about eight feet across and deep enough for Rudy and Digger to stand up straight. Clancy even dragged an old rug out of his basement and put it on the dirt floor. When we tired of digging on hot afternoons, we gathered there in the black coolness and listened to Digger review his latest theories on his favorite subject.

Unfortunately the ice wagon came along to interrupt our progress. The ice man came twice a week to fill the wooden boxes most everyone used. Mister Westrup, the one-armed delivery man, drove his horse-drawn wagon through the streets shouting, "Ice," and all the kids and dogs stopped whatever they were doing and chased the wagon. We all wanted to make off with a piece of ice too small to sell. Blackie loved ice. Mister Westrup acted like he was against it, sometimes he even whacked us across the hand, but then he laughed about it.

He never wore a shirt in summer, only a leather shoulder apron, and the amputated left forearm made him look like a pirate. The good arm had a tattoo of a naked lady that Digger claimed showed everything. But it was impossible to get a good look with his muscle always flexing. He'd hoist a big block with metal tongs, bring it to rest on his shoulder, then steady it with the stub. We'd cheer him on, knowing that as soon as he left we could fill our pockets.

But on this day Westrup was in a lousy mood. He was parked in front of Clancy's house, and he stood up in the wagon and yelled, "Listen, you kids." He waited for the noise to stop. "The company put some new chemical in the ice to make it last longer. It'll make you sick. Understand? So don't touch it." He slid off the wagon, then picked up a block of ice and threw it on his shoulder. "If you get sick, it's not my fault." He turned and walked up Clancy's sidewalk toward the house.

We watched him until he turned a corner. "Won't make me sick," said Digger. He grabbed a chunk and bit off a piece.

"Me neither," said Rudy.

"Nothing makes me sick," said Dunster. Digger looked at me, hoping that wasn't true. Everyone took a piece, including Mary Lou. I took a piece just as Mister

Westrup came around the corner.

"I saw that!" he yelled. He waved the tongs. "Now get out of here." We ran off laughing and hooting.

It didn't take long. By late afternoon, Clancy, Bernie, and I were the only kids left at the lot. Digger ran home an hour earlier, and Rudy an hour before that. I was beginning to feel a little peculiar. The sun felt like it was burning into my head, the light was blinding, and suddenly I felt awful. "See you guys," I said, then staggered home. Mary Lou was already in the bathroom when I arrived. We were sick that night and all the following day. I made it out the next day, even though Mary Lou was still in bed. Bernie was the only one there at the lot.

"Didn't you get sick?" I said.

Bernie pulled out a Baby Ruth bar, unwrapped it, and began picking at it with his filthy fingers. "I never get sick." When he offered me some, I turned it down. I still wasn't too sure of myself.

But I'd given the ice a lot of thought. It had real possibilities for school, the very thing Maxie Grover and the rest of us were looking for.

By Monday, everyone was back except Rudy who had been extra greedy with the ice. Clancy and Digger looked pale, but the old fire was back.

Clancy started off with a great idea. "Why not dig a secret room beneath the club room?" The plan was to dig a hole in the existing floor, then cover it with an old, wooden gate he'd found. The rug would cover the gate and no one would know it was there, including Bernie. But it had to be dug in secret. I asked whether that was fair to Bernie, but Digger said we shouldn't feel guilty since Bernie was the only one initiated. We all agreed. So much for fair play.

We worked on it in the evenings, and digging wasn't as hard as hauling out the dirt. After three days we'd finished a hole Rudy could almost stand up in. The rug covered the gate perfectly, and there was no hint of what was underneath.

The hidden room opened up all kinds of possibilities. We'd do anything to stir up a chase, then dive into the closest tunnel, crawl to the great chamber, lift up the rug and gate, drop into the hole, and then let the lid fall. It was slick and easy. Immediately we were famous for our disappearing act. We could have cashed in all kinds of marbles, frogs, and baseball cards, if we'd been willing to share the secret.

Clancy insisted on using a candle, like coal miners, to make sure the air was good enough to support combustion. Digger and I had no idea what that meant, but we figured Clancy was right.

The hole was a great place to catch up on the latest gossip. Pursuers normally ended up in the room above, and we could hear everything, with only the rug and gate separating us.

One morning Digger and I spotted Dunster and Mary Lou playing hopscotch on the sidewalk in front of the monkey tree. They were arguing and didn't notice us coming out from one of the tunnels. We were tired of digging and were looking for some excitement.

"Let's get Dunster and Mary Lou to chase us," I said.

"Are you kidding?" said Digger.

"Why not? It's a chance to get back at Dunster. She'll never find us."

"Anyone but Dunster," he mumbled.

"All right, I'll do it without you." I took off.

"Wait a minute!" said Digger. "What're you gonna do?"

I turned around. "What do you care?"

"Just curious."

I walked back. "Look. Dunster has this flat rock. Says it brings her good luck playing hopscotch. It drives Mary Lou crazy. Anyway, I could hide in the weeds and when the time's right run out and grab it, then run for the chamber."

"You're crazy," said Digger. "You'll never make it. Dunster's fast. She'll kill you."

"Got a better idea?" I said.

He shrugged.

"Why don't you wait here on this side of the street. I'll snatch the rock and throw it to you. Then we'll run for different tunnels."

He licked his lips. "That could work."

Digger hid in a patch of weeds close to the street, while I ran back to the alley, through Clancy's yard, and circled around from behind. I could hear Dunster and Mary Lou talking as I crawled through the weeds behind the monkey tree. But instead of staying in the weeds, I climbed the second tree, crossed to the first on the cables, and studied them from the platform. Mary Lou and Dunster were directly below. I held the cable swing and waited for the right moment.

Dunster threw her lucky rock and it landed on a line. "No good," shouted Mary Lou.

"What do you mean?" shouted Dunster. "It's a five."

"No it isn't!" shouted Mary Lou.

I swung down, hit the ground running, snatched the rock, took off, then threw it as hard as I could. It was a lousy throw. The rock went high and landed in the street. Digger popped out of the weeds, ran out and grabbed it, then headed for the tunnels.

"Get 'em!" screamed Dunster, but I was already halfway across the street. I dropped in a tunnel entrance, then took off on all fours. On the last turn before the great room, my head hit something round and hard. Clancy's head.

"Holy shit!" screamed Clancy. He held his head. "What are you doing here?"

"Dunster's after us!"

"Geez," he mumbled. He turned and headed back to the club room with me right behind. It was dark, but we knew the tunnels by heart.

"What took you so long?" said Digger. He was standing in the chamber with the lid up. Sunlight from the small hole in the roof took the edge off the darkness.

Clancy dropped in and I followed. Digger let the lid fall in place.

"That was close," I said. I was breathing hard and so were the other two.

"Quiet!" said Clancy. "Don't waste the air. Now who's got the candle?"

"Got it," said Digger. He struck a match and lit the candle. We sat back, listening.

Dunster and Mary Lou shouted back and forth. Their voices echoed through the tunnels. Someone even crawled over the lid, but they didn't stop. When we were sure they were some distance away, we opened the lid for some fresh air. The candle flame came alive.

We dropped the lid and settled back. Soon we heard someone coming.

"Pretty neat," said Mary Lou. Her voice was loud, clear. "A rug and everything."

"Let's rest a minute," said Dunster. We could hear them shuffling on the carpet above.

"Wish we had a flashlight," said Mary Lou. "That hole in the ceiling doesn't do much."

"Where do you suppose they went?" said Dunster. "If I get my hands on Digger, I'll kill him." Digger glanced up. His eyes were large. "Haven't got him for a long time," she said.

"Think you'll ever stop?" said Mary Lou.

"Never," said Dunster. Digger looked away.

"What was that?" asked Mary Lou.

"A dog," said Dunster.

"It's Blackie," mouthed Digger. He pointed with his thumb. We heard more movement above.

"Oh, that's a nice boy," said Dunster. Then we heard Blackie's loving whimpers.

"I thought Blackie hated the tunnels," I whispered.

"He does," whispered Digger. His lips disappeared.

Clancy put a finger to his lips. "Shh."

"Oh, that's a nice Blackie," said Dunster. "Bet you want a nice piece of chocolate."

"Jeez," whispered Clancy.

"Great dog you got there," I said. Digger didn't answer.

Suddenly Blackie started scratching at the rug. "What's wrong with him?" said Mary Lou.

"Beats me," said Dunster.

"They're gonna find us," I whispered. Digger looked frantic.

"What's he looking for?" said Mary Lou.

"Maybe he has to go," said Dunster. "Wouldn't that be perfect?"

"Let's get out of here," said Mary Lou.

The voices faded while Blackie kept barking and scratching at the rug. When Clancy said it was safe, Digger pushed up the lid and Blackie went nuts. He charged into the wall, backed off, then hit it again. When he found an opening, he ran off barking and whining.

"Blackie found Digger!" echoed Dunster's voice.

"Let's go!" said Clancy. We took off in the opposite

direction. Digger ran over me, and when I surfaced he was halfway to the monkey tree. It was a good idea. No one could trap us there.

When I pulled myself up, Clancy and Digger were sitting on the platform trying to catch their breath.

"That dog of yours," said Clancy. He shook his head. "Didn't even recognize you."

Digger didn't answer. He was thinking about Dunster.

We waited a long time before Mary Lou came out of a tunnel. I knew something was wrong. She looked around, and when she spotted us she shouted. "You guys have to help. Dunster's been hurt."

Digger looked at me. "No way," he mumbled.

"What happened?" I shouted.

"Dunster fell in this hole," she yelled.

Clancy spun around and glared at Digger. "You dumb shit, didn't you put the lid down?"

"I was in a hurry," said Digger. He shrugged.

"We better help," I said, then stood and grabbed the swing.

"All right," said Clancy. Digger pulled his knees tight in against his chest. I swung to the ground and Clancy followed.

Mary Lou looked anxious. "She's hurt bad," she said. It could have been a ploy, but Mary Lou wasn't good at acting.

Dunster's head appeared at the tunnel entrance and Clancy and I helped her crawl out. We took only a few steps before Mary Lou pushed me away. "I can take her from here," she said.

We watched Dunster hop down the street on one foot. When we looked up at Digger, he was grinning like a snake in sunshine.

"Let's cover up the chamber," I said, "before some-one else comes along."

"Won't do any good," said Clancy. "The word's out."

"I'll talk to Mary Lou. They'll keep mum."

"Why would they?"

"Because they can use it, too."

"Yeah. That's right." he said. He looked off nodding his head.

At lunch Mary Lou said Dunster had a broken foot. When I told Digger, he made no comment. But he was giddy the rest of the day.

TWENTY-THREE

Clancy got a new bicycle, and in no time we all knew how to ride it. He was good about letting us take turns. While one was riding, the others gave chase. The goal was to stop the rider. That's what we were doing that evening when we spotted the black Packard in front of the Turk's house. Rudy was riding the bike, and we stopped her two doors down the street.

"I'm sure it's them," said Digger.

"Horse shit," said Rudy. It was her first turn on the bike and she wanted to continue.

"What are they doing there?" said Clancy.

"It could be someone else," I said. I was still studying the car.

"Let's find out," said Clancy. He took off on his bike, and we chased him through my yard into the alley. He dropped off the bike, then we approached the Turk's house from the Beans' rear yard, which was dangerous in itself.

The Turk's lighted living room windows were too high for us to see in, so we had to climb the tree at the corner of the house. The tree was hard to get to because of high bushes, but they gave good cover from the street.

Rudy was the first one in the tree, and she moved up fast. "He's in there," she whispered. Her face was lit by the light from the window. Clancy and I scrambled up to her level.

"Yeah," said Clancy. "It's them all right. Three of 'em, and the Turk."

I was surprised at how nice the room was. There were large paintings on the wall and a grand piano in one corner. The Turk sat alone on a couch and didn't look that happy. Three men stood off to one side talking; the tallest one walked over and shouted at the Turk. Finally he shook his fist, and the Turk turned away. That really got him mad because he grabbed the Turk and pulled him out of his chair. That was the last thing I saw because someone slammed a car door and we were on the ground in seconds.

"It's the guy who washes the car," whispered Digger, pointing with his thumb. Digger had been waiting in the bushes because there wasn't room for him in the tree. We peered through the growth and saw the man standing by the car. He lit a cigarette, looked straight at where we were, then walked around to the other side and leaned against the hood.

"Let's go," I said. We slipped out of the bushes, ran down the Beans' side yard, crossed the alley, and headed for the park. Rudy got there first.

"What do you think?" said Clancy. He plopped down

next to Rudy and me. Digger finally arrived.

"Don't know," I said. "But it looks su-suspi-"

"Suspicious," said Clancy. He wasn't patient with anyone slower, which included every kid in the neighborhood except Bernie. "Wonder what the Turk did?"

"They were mad about something," I said. Digger was still breathing too hard to say anything.

"And that big guy looked mean," said Clancy.

Rudy scratched her cheek. "The Turk could take him."

We all agreed.

"Maybe that's why the Turk keeps stuff buried in the back yard," I said.

We talked until dark.

When I arrived home, I found my father in the living room in his favorite chair, a Zane Grey novel in his hand. He was asleep. I touched his arm and his eyes opened. He studied me for a moment, then lifted me as if I weighed nothing and placed me beside him. He smelled of aftershave.

"Where have you been?" he said. I liked it when I had him all to myself.

"Out with my friends," I said.

"Isn't it time for bed?"

"Not yet." I looked up and noticed the wrinkles around his eyes. He looked tired.

"All right." He said. I could feel the warmth of his breath. "What's on your mind?"

"It's the Turk," I said.

"The Turk?" He leaned back. "Where have you been?"

"Just walking past his house. There was a black car out front."

"And?"

"We stopped and looked inside."

He considered that. "You couldn't see anything from the street."

"We climbed a tree."

"Maybe you better tell me everything."

I did, and reminded him about seeing the Turk digging in his back yard. I didn't mention leaving a note in the can. He wouldn't have liked that. "Why are those men mad at him?"

"I hate to think he's doing business with them." He rubbed his eyes with his thumb and forefinger. "I want you to stay away from there. Understand? Also, the house on the corner. Those men are no good."

"Yes, sir," I said.

He squeezed me hard and held me for a long time. That night I couldn't sleep. All I could think about was the expression on the Turk's face.

The following day we heard the news about Bernie Heifitz. We were sorry we weren't around when the ambulance came and took him to the hospital. My mother was stunned. It was polio. The sickness everyone feared. She gave Mary Lou and me a bath even though it was only Wednesday. I hadn't seen Bernie for over a week, but that didn't seem to matter. "You might have touched something he touched," she said.

Bernie's mother stopped her noon-time call. I realized something important was missing from the neighborhood. A week passed before news came that Bernie wasn't expected to live. Mothers talked for hours over back fences, and kids were instructed to stay away from Bernie's house. No one even played with Bernie's sister. Mrs. Bean surprised everyone and took soup and fresh rolls to their house. Then everyone joined in with casseroles and cakes. There was nothing to do but wait.

Two more days passed, then the final news. Bernie was going to make it. Everyone was jubilant, though they wondered whether he'd be able to walk. No one dared ask Mrs. Heifitz.

Mary Lou and I were now scrubbed morning and night, and another scrubbing was added at noon along with an increase in tomato soup. Mother was going to keep us healthy if it killed us.

I thought of the time we dripped hot wax on Bernie's chest and wished it had never happened. I wasn't the only one. We talked about it a lot.

Neighborhood wars were in full swing by midsummer. It started when a gang of nine-year-olds from the south took over the park. They extorted marbles from younger kids every time they used the swings and teeter-totter. Someone was always there to make collections. They never bothered us, since we were too close to the same age. But something had to be done.

We attempted a couple of ambushes, hoping to get the marbles back, but none succeeded. By then they knew who we were, and word spread they were out to get us.

One afternoon we spotted five of the bad guys sitting under the largest tree in the park counting their take for the day.

"Let's get 'em," said Digger.

"Smart," said Clancy. "Five of them—three of us."

Digger licked his lips, his eyes were narrow slits. "Got an idea," he said. And it was good. We ran to the tennis court, filled our pockets with gravel from under a bench, then ran back and climbed to the roof of the equipment shed. The same place Digger's fiasco with Dunster occurred the summer before. We clearly controlled the high ground, but the enemy was out of range.

"What do we do now?" I said.

"I'll take care of that," said Digger, in a deep voice that mimicked Tom Mix on the radio. He chuckled as he waved his hands. "Hey, you guys! Want some marbles?"

The troublemakers stopped counting and looked up. The largest, ugliest, and meanest stood up and shouted. "Sure. Why not!" He motioned for the others to follow and started toward us. I wondered whether we'd made a terrible mistake.

They gathered below us, no more than ten feet

away. "Still want some marbles?" Digger yelled.

"Yeah," said Big and Ugly. He was grinning like he'd already made a heist.

"Here they are!" screamed Digger and let them have it with a volley of rocks. We joined in, and they scrambled around like they were chasing quarters until the pain of being hit stopped them.

Big and Ugly yelled for a retreat, then shouted over his shoulder, "We'll get you bastards!" One of them dropped a sack of marbles. Quick as a cat, Clancy leaped from the roof, snatched the sack of marbles, and took off.

"Come on!" he shouted. A smart move. We were almost out of rocks. Digger and I hit the ground running and the bad guys came after us.

"The tunnels!" shouted Clancy. He was halfway across the street. Of course, the tunnels. Why hadn't I thought of it?

Digger and I shot into the first hole, crawled to the great room, and found Clancy standing in the sub-chamber with the lid up. We slipped in, Clancy dropped the lid, and we sat back still panting. Nothing was heard for a long time. Clancy lifted the lid, and we all took a deep breath. He dropped the lid again and Digger lit a candle.

The bad guys took a long time before they gathered in the great room. We were tired and stiff from sitting hunched up and squeezed together. Then we had to listen to what they planned to do with "the marble snatchers." Big and Ugly laughed, and it sounded sinister. I wondered if there was any hope. They talked for a long time.

"We could suffocate down here," whispered Clancy. The flame flickered. "We're going to die. Either down here or up there." He pointed with his thumb.

"They'll torture us," said Digger, louder than he should have.

"What was that?" came a voice from above.

"What do you mean?" This time it was Big and Ugly.

"I thought I heard something."

"You're getting spooked," said Big and Ugly.

"No, really, just listen."

The candle went out. Clancy whispered so softly I could scarcely hear him. "Let's put our backs up against the lid. And when I count to three we'll push up. It'll scare the hell out of 'em."

"Jesus," moaned Digger.

"What was that?" came the voice again.

"What else can we do?" I whispered.

"I heard it that time!" said Big and Ugly.

"When I say three, push up and scream your guts out," whispered Clancy. We placed our backs against the plywood. "One. Two. Three. YAAAHHHH!" The lid flew back.

And there they were! Screaming! Howling! Big and Ugly plunged head first through the roof. Sunlight poured in the big hole. The other four practically killed each other following him out.

Digger poked his head through the hole and described the retreat. He dropped back down grinning so hard his lip cracked and started to bleed. "Guess they need a change of underwear," he said. We laughed.

"Let's get out of here," said Clancy. "They'll be back."

"Too bad," I said. "That's the end of the hideout."

"Yep" said Clancy. "We'll have to figure out something else." He climbed out the hole in the roof.

Big and Ugly and his gang were back in half an hour, but this time Grumble and Mike, along with some other older kids, were there to greet them. It was a stand-off. Big and Ugly told Grumble they'd get us sooner or later. Grumble told him to stick it.

TWENTY - FOUR

I made all kinds of promises I knew I couldn't keep to get my father to buy me a bike. It was bright red and wasn't as nice or expensive as Clancy's, but it was good enough. The first day Clancy and I went for a long ride down a country road. There wasn't a cloud in the sky, and a soft, cool wind was coming off the lake. We turned down a gravel road with tomato fields on both sides.

"I feel sorry for Bernie," said Clancy. "I'd hate to spend every day in bed."

"Will he ever walk again?"

"My mom says he will, but maybe with a brace. At least he won't be tagging along."

"That's too bad," Clancy said. "But the guy was always getting caught."

To be fair to Bernie, that day swiping tomatoes was a close call for all of us. Particularly me. Our system was simple. We ran down the rows picking, then filling our shirt tails until they were bulging. We could still run with the load high and out front, and that's what we were doing when this farmer spotted us. Normally they were fat and old, but this guy was young, the fastest I'd ever seen.

Digger jumped a wire fence with a full load. I followed, but my toe snagged and spilled me forward. I hit flat on my stomach, crushing the whole load of tomatoes. Squish! I rolled to my feet and ran. Digger said it looked like I'd flopped on a grenade.

I ran home and tried to sneak through the kitchen, but my mother was standing at the sink. She screamed. Then went out of her head.

"I'm all right!" I yelled. "Just tomatoes!" It took ten minutes to calm her down.

Old Bernie was caught red-handed, and he spilled the beans on all of us. The farmer told him he was going to call the police. Then he backed off after Bernie promised never to return. That took one whole field out. Repeat that a few times and we'd have been out of business.

We turned on to a dirt road, and Clancy stood up pumping and took off. He wanted a race. I came off the seat, pumping hard. We passed through the tomato fields and entered the marshlands bordering the river. The dirt road was narrow and dusty. Low trees and bushes flashed past. I barely caught up to Clancy when suddenly we were flying through the air upside-down, our bikes somersaulting over us. We landed hard on gravel.

"Holy shit," mumbled Clancy. "What happened?"

I could hardly see through the dust. My back ached

and my eyes burned. I pulled myself up and watched two older guys withdraw sticks from the spokes of our front wheels. I looked at Clancy. It was clear what they'd done.

The biggest guy grabbed me and punched me in the stomach. The other one latched on to Clancy.

"Okay you guys!" yelled the big one. "Don't try to get away!" He twisted my arm behind my back.

I'd seen them before at school. They were from the neighborhood to the south. We were in a lot of trouble.

They forced us to stand up, then pushed us into the low, dense growth at the side of the road. The sun felt hot, weeds cut at my legs, and I was sweating as we headed for the river. Grumble had once brought us here, but he acted nervous. It was definitely not our territory. He wanted to show us the old bridge everyone talked about.

We drew closer to the river. I heard voices off in the distance. Then I spotted the bridge abutment and the steel framework looming out of the brush. The shouting grew louder, then suddenly stopped. It was eerie. I looked at Clancy and I could tell he was thinking hard. The two guys made us stop, then stood on their toes, trying to see something in the distance. A loud voice sounded. "READY. AIM. FIRE!" BB guns fired slightly out of unison. Someone screamed.

"The firing squad," mouthed Clancy. Grumble had told us about it, but, like most things, we didn't believe him.

Clancy took several deep breaths. Then exploded. He thrashed around like a maniac. Before I knew it, the guy guarding him was on the ground and Clancy was off like a trap-sprung rat. The guy holding me ran after him, but the jerk on the ground grabbed my ankle. A kick in the ribs settled him. I plunged into a thicket and crashed through dead branches until I came out in a wide, grassy meadow. There, only a half-football field away, was the firing squad!

A skinny redhead held what had to be his father's sabre, while the firing squad loaded their BB guns. The same guys we took the marbles from. Big and Ugly was there. Then I spotted Digger. He was standing alone against the bridge abutment, hands tied behind his back. Blindfolded. The next victim. I turned to run and crashed into the jerk coming after me. We fell to the ground. I was up and away before he knew what hit him.

I dove into the undergrowth, then crawled on hands and knees through more twisted reeds and muck. "He's over here!" screamed the guy I just nailed. I could hear him coming through the thicket not far behind. Scratches on my arms and legs stung from dirty water and muck.

I entered a meadow filled with thick, high grass, still in view of the bridge. I was trapped. Everyone, including the firing squad, was coming after me. The tall grass was my only hope. I dropped to my knees and crawled at a speed I could never duplicate, then realized I was going in circles. I rolled over on my back and tunneled through the weeds, gulping air and looking into a blinding sun.

The bastards walked back and forth, flaying the grass and screaming. They were only a few feet away. One even stepped on my finger. All I thought about was how bad a BB could hurt. But they didn't see me. It was a miracle.

Finally the redhead with the sabre called them back. I lay back and tried to catch my breath. The weeds gave little shade, and I was so hot and exhausted I almost didn't care.

It wasn't long before the redhead shouted, "Are you ready?"

"Yes sir!" came a loud reply.

I sat up to see what was happening. The fields shimmered in the morning heat and the sun drained the color from everything. A kid stood to the side of Digger, making him stand up straight with his back to the line of guns.

"READY. AIM. FIRE!" Rifles cracked and Digger screamed. He bent forward. I lay back down and looked up at the sky. Me next?

The shouting increased. "Get him!" they screamed.

I raised up and saw Digger running. The firing squad was hot on his tail. Somehow he'd broken loose. I was jubilant. But not for long. Digger was headed directly for me. I had to worry about being trampled.

I even half stood and tried to wave him off. "Not

this way!" He had the entire field but it was no use. He kept coming, whimpering and groaning, then tripped over me.

I don't remember what I said, but it must have been inspiring. He jumped up and took off like Charlie Chaplin in fast forward. And I was right behind. No one was going to catch Digger, or me for that matter. We raced through the heaviest thicket, then across a large tomato field. When we arrived at the park we could hardly breathe.

We sat down under a tree and looked at the wound in Digger's calf. It didn't look that bad. There was a deep dent, and it was black and blue, but practically no blood. We lay there a long time and bragged and hooted until what was said lost all touch with reality.

We could have bragged even more if Digger hadn't been careless. On the way home, Dunster nailed him. She was reading in her favorite tree, and he just made it easy. It demeaned the whole affair. Sometimes Digger showed no more sense than old Blackie.

The following morning, Clancy and I found our bikes dangling from the flagpole at school, exactly where we thought they'd be. But that wasn't a big deal. We got the janitor to pull them down. All things considered, we came out all right. Two spokes on Clancy's bike and one on mine.

TWENTY-FIVE

I awakened early and decided to look for Digger. I needed to fire him up about the Beans' yard. It had been spared too long. I quickly dressed, slipped out the back door, raced across the lawn, turned the corner behind the garage, and smacked head on into a man. I was more surprised than frightened as I looked up into a familiar face. It was Ernie. He grabbed me by the shoulders and held me at bay.

"Wait a minute," he said, dragging it out. "Where you off to, fella?" He was grinning.

"Sorry," I said.

"Better be careful," he said, then let me go.

"I didn't see you," I said.

"Just don't let it happen again." He chuckled. New bib overalls made him look more prosperous than the year before.

"What are you doing here?" I said.

"I work for a man who lives in that house." He pointed.

"You mean the Turk?"

"Hah. You call him the Turk?" He looked away,

smiling. "That's a good one. He's no Turk. He's a Cypriot."

"What's that?"

"It doesn't matter." He waved it off.

"What do you do?" I said.

"Water the grapes. Weed a little. Mow the lawn."

"He's a strange man," I said.

"A nice man," said Ernie. "Very nice. He helps a lot of people." He motioned for me to walk along.

"Why does he do that?" I said.

"He was down on his luck once and knows what it's like. I better hurry. He doesn't like me to be late." Ernie unlocked the gate, waved, then slipped inside.

I tried to see if the Turk was waiting for him, but the gate slammed shut before I had a chance.

I met Digger coming out of his back door and told him about meeting Ernie, but my explanation wasn't good enough. He had to find out for himself. The Beans' yard was postponed for another day.

We ran back to the Turk's fence, and Digger took the knothole. "Can you see anything?" I was looking through the slit.

"Not much," he said. He looked around, nodded toward Clancy's garage, then wiped his nose with the inside of his wrist. An old rose trellis made the garage roof easily accessible, so Digger went up, and I followed. Ernie was installing some metal grillwork on a basement window, and the Turk was there talking to him. We watched them until the Turk glanced up.

He looked angry.

"Let's get out of here," said Digger. He slid to the edge of the roof and dropped off. I crawled back down the trellis.

"I don't think Ernie wants us around," Digger said.

"You're quick," I said.

He shrugged. "So what should we do?"

"What about Beans' yard?"

"It's too late. Dunster will be around."

I was disappointed. "Guess I'll go home for breakfast."

"What are you having?"

"Orange juice and oatmeal." I never mentioned cod liver oil, even to close friends. "Come on. There's plenty."

He thought about it. "Yeah, well, see you at the park." He broke wind, then turned and walked off.

Digger's calf wound festered and turned a greenish-purple. His mother put on a fresh bandage every morning, which seldom lasted into the afternoon. It was a constant reminder of the firing squad. And got to be an obsession with Clancy and me.

"We just escaped," I said. "We never got back at anybody."

"That's right," said Clancy. "We've got to get those guys. Three spokes. And look what they did to Digger."

"It's terrible," lisped Rudy. She never really saw the wound. Whenever Digger pulled back the bandage, she looked the other way.

"Wonder if those guys have a hideout?" I said.

"We could destroy it," said Clancy.

"What about their swimming hole," said Rudy. We all looked at her. "Old Slippery Ass." The combination left moisture on our faces.

"Right," said Clancy. "Grumble told us about it."

"We've never been there," I said.

"They go swimming without suits," said Digger. He chuckled. "Would I like to find that."

"Me, too," said Clancy.

"Yeah," said Rudy.

"I'll bet you would," said Digger, grinning. Rudy returned a vicious look. She didn't speak to him the rest of the day. Digger felt bad about it, but there was no use apologizing. Rudy was becoming more sensitive. It had been coming on for some time.

That evening we went in search of Grumble to get more information on the swimming hole. We had to be careful. The gang from the south was older, larger, and traveled in groups of five or more. And then there was the firing squad.

It took us an hour before we found Grumble and Mike behind Clancy's garage. Grumble held a rope with one end already tied in a noose, and Mike held a struggling cat with one watery eye. We were interrupting a hanging, though they denied it.

Grumble draped the rope around his neck. "What do you want?"

"How far is Old Slippery Ass?" said Digger.

Grumble thought for a moment, his nose wrinkled, forcing one eye shut. "Not far," he said. He picked up a stick and drew a diagram in the dirt. "You just go to the bridge, cross it, then move along the river, and it's right there." He dug a hole with the stick.

Mike handed Rudy the cat and picked up another stick. "There's a big clump of trees right there," he said. "It's just on the other side."

Rudy slipped away to the corner of the garage and let the cat go.

"What about crossing the bridge?" said Clancy.

"Easy," said Grumble. "You'll figure it out once you get there."

"Thanks," said Digger.

"What's the big deal?" said Grumble.

Digger pulled back the bandage. "See what they did? We want to get 'em."

"The firing squad?" said Mike. He knelt down for a closer look.

"Those bastards," said Grumble. He studied the wound, then looked up. "Better be careful."

Digger plastered down the bandage. "We will," he said.

"Wait a minute!" shouted Mike. He jumped up and looked around. "Where's the cat?" He glared at Rudy.

"I don't know," said Rudy. Her face was calm, her eyes ice cold. She was already twice as smart as her brother.

"Dummy!" screamed Grumble. "You let it get away!"

"Wasn't me!" shouted Mike.

We left them screaming at each other. On the way back to the park, the black Packard pulled up and stopped in front of us as we crossed the street. The driver rolled down the window and acted like he wanted to talk to us. Clancy turned and ran back across the street. We raced after him into his back yard.

"What did he want?" said Digger.

"My dad told me to stay away from those men," said Clancy.

"So did mine," I said.

It was the first time the driver made any attempt to talk to us. He looked friendly enough. We wondered what it meant. We ran around the other side of the house and stopped behind some bushes. The car was gone.

T W E N T Y - S I X

We met at the park the following morning and spent a lot of time huffing and puffing about what we were going to do once we found the bad guys. Rudy didn't show up. Digger, Clancy, and I left for the river without her. I figured it was more fear than anger that kept her away.

Blackie was also with us, sniffing around, probably looking forward to another day of hunting, but Clancy insisted he stay behind. Blackie's day hadn't been wasted. He'd already done the job on the Beans' lawn, which was all he was really good at.

The morning was sunny, sticky, the air filled with insects fattened in the summer swamp. We moved cautiously across the first open meadow, then descended into the thicket that filled the marshlands. No oaks grew here, only poplars and willows. The path was narrow, winding, the ground soggy. Our feet were soaked in no time. When we finally emerged from the thicket, we were only a short distance from the concrete buttress of the bridge. We looked around before entering the clearing.

Digger pointed out the spot where he stood before the firing squad. "Right here," he said. "I had my face to the wall." He grimaced. "Those bastards." Again I was filled with hate and loathing.

Clancy wasn't paying attention. He was trying to figure out how to cross the bridge. Grumble said it was easy, but it didn't look that way to me. The bridge was a steel frame with diagonal braces supported by a concrete buttress at either end. From the side it looked like a finished bridge, but there were only a few steel braces where the roadbed should have been. It was another project left uncompleted because of the Depression.

"Guess we're supposed to walk on the steel beams," said Clancy. His face was red, his forehead dotted with sweat.

"Are you kidding?" I said. It looked impossible.

"Got a better idea?" said Digger.

"Watch it," whispered Clancy. "Over there." He pointed, then slipped into the stinking undergrowth. We followed.

Two kids came strolling down the path. They crawled the abutment, then stood for a moment and looked around. It was the redhead.

"The guy with the sword," whispered Digger so softly I could scarcely hear him.

"I know."

"We'll follow them," whispered Clancy. He was chewing a weed and squinting. We watched as the two moved easily along the bottom beam, clinging to the cross bracing. When they arrived at the other side they jumped from the abutment and disappeared into the brush. We waited, swatting mosquitoes. The sun was higher, and the moist air stuck to us like wet sand.

Climbing the buttress was easy. There were steel rungs we hadn't noticed before. And once on top I looked around at the view. The bottom beam of the truss, high above the water, looked wide enough to walk on. And there was more than enough bracing to hang on to. But the rusty metal was hot from the sun.

Clancy went first, I followed, and it wasn't bad except for looking down. The river was shallow, murky, an open sewer. Despite the smell, it held a certain romance. We arrived on the other side and I glanced back to make sure I understood everything in case of a quick retreat. I wondered if we were making a terrible mistake.

Clancy jumped off the abutment, which wasn't far from the ground. Digger and I followed. We were deep in enemy territory now. Clancy spotted the path and we continued along the river. Weeds and bulrushes walled us in on either side.

"This is easy," said Clancy, but his voice broke.

"Yeah," I said. I didn't mean it either.

"Quiet," said Digger.

Above the weeds to our right, we could see the tops of the trees Mike told us about. And it wasn't long before we could hear the shouts of the enemy at play.

"What do we do now?" said Digger. He acted like he wanted to leave. I know I did.

"Let's get off the path," said Clancy. He stepped into the brush and we followed. The sound of laughter grew louder, and through the undergrowth I could see the sparkle of sun on the water. Clancy stopped me with a stiff arm. Digger plowed into my back.

"There they are," whispered Clancy. He hunkered down and parted the branches of a bush.

"Where?" said Digger.

"Down!" said Clancy.

I dropped behind another bush and pushed aside the foliage. And there was Old Slippery Ass, like a picture in a travel book. Huge poplars surrounded the pond, their limbs extended low over black, green water. The abandoned brick quarry looked completely natural, like it had been there for a thousand years. Naked bodies slid down wet, clay banks, hung from branches, leaped out of trees. They laughed, splashed, frolicked, and swore. Even their fannies were tan, except for the redhead who was red all over.

"Looks like fun," I whispered.

"Yeah," said Digger. "If you can swim."

"I can," said Clancy and I in unison. We locked little fingers and shook on it.

"Not me," said Digger. I stared in disbelief but decided not to push it.

"Let's wait till they go, then give her a try," said Clancy. He looked like he had just won a game of marbles.

"Not me," said Digger.

"Maybe we should go," I said.

Clancy groaned. "We've got to try it sometime."

We crawled back to the path and ran until we reached the bridge. Digger's speed was amazing.

Once across the bridge and out of the swamp, we ran all the way back to the park. It was just before lunch and Rudy was there. She looked glad to see us.

"Where you been?" she said.

"Old Slippery Ass," said Digger. They were talking again.

"Was it nifty?"

"Yeah," said Clancy. "We're going back tomorrow. You've gotta see it. We've got a plan."

"Not my plan," said Digger. He folded his arms and stuck out his chin.

"It could really work," said Clancy.

"I'm for it," I said. Digger looked away. Clancy explained the plan to Rudy while Digger chewed on a fingernail. Digger didn't like the part that involved Dunster.

"What do you think?" said Clancy.

"It's all right," Rudy said. She looked off, nodding, her lower lip extended.

"I'm not going," said Digger.

"Come on," I said. "You're just scared of Dunster."

"No, I'm not." His eyes blazed. "What makes you think she'll do it, anyway?"

"What does she have to lose?" I said.

Clancy frowned. "Let's ask her, okay?"

"Go ahead," said Digger. "But without me."

"Okay, without you," said Clancy.

"See you." Digger called Blackie, then headed for home, but, as usual, Blackie didn't follow. I felt sorry for Digger. We watched him until he turned the corner at Clancy's house.

There was no question of where to look for Dunster. She spent most of her time in a large sycamore reading Nancy Drew and munching whatever fruit was in season and easily swiped. She could eat green apples all day. The tree was in the parking strip in front of Bernie Heifitz's house. Unless Digger took a detour, which he always did now, he'd have to pass right underneath it on the way home.

Clancy, Rudy, and I swiped some apples from Beckman's back yard for a peace offering, then proceeded to the base of the tree. We sat down, leaned against the trunk, and munched on the apples as loud as we could. They were too sour. We waited.

"Okay, Dunster!" I shouted. "We know you're up there." No answer. We expected that.

"Come on," said Clancy. "We haven't got all day."

A pair of thick, horn-rimmed glasses landed in the grass in front of us. Dunster's, of course. "Shit," a voice sounded from high in the tree. In seconds a tall, thin figure, book in hand, swung down from the lowest branch and landed in front of us. In the trees Dunster was almost as graceful as Rudy.

"Damn it," she said. "See what you made me do." She dropped to her knees and groped around for her glasses.

"Wasn't our fault," said Clancy, then handed her the glasses. She snatched them away and squinted as she checked to see if anything was broken. I had no idea her eyesight was that bad.

"What do you want?" she said.

"Got an idea," said Clancy.

"You'll like it," I added quickly.

She snatched one of my apples and took a big bite. Rudy winced. Dunster had a cast iron stomach. "What is it?"

Clancy quickly explained the details of his plan. Dunster's mouth turned up at the corners. It was the closest she ever came to a smile. She threw the apple core over her shoulder.

"You'll do it?" said Clancy.

She grabbed another apple. "Sure, why not?" Another big bite. Rudy puckered up and turned away.

"Great," said Clancy. "If we can get Grumble and Mike, we'll do it tomorrow."

"I'll be here," said Dunster.

"Want any more of these apples?" I said.

"Just put 'em there." She pointed to the base of the tree. With an apple and book in one hand, she swung easily into the tree. Rolling forward, her long arm swung around and she grabbed a higher branch. Her tennis shoes conformed to the trunk like hands as she ascended in clean, easy moves. Maybe she was better than Rudy? In seconds she was lost in the leaves.

After lunch we found Grumble and Mike working on their go-cart, and, as usual, they were arguing. It was a project they'd been working on all summer but couldn't seem to finish. They even admitted it was ugly, but what more could you do with an orange crate? We presented our plan and both agreed to join us. They didn't even have any suggestions. This wasn't like Grumble at all. We returned to the park and reported the good news to Digger. He still didn't want to discuss it.

TWENTY-SEVEN

First thing the next morning, Rudy went to find Dunster and I went after Grumble and Mike. Pulling them away from their go-cart wasn't easy. It was just about ready to try out. I had to remind them of their promise. Everyone finally gathered at the park. Digger refused to get anywhere near Dunster. Old Blackie snuggled up to her and licked her hand. Digger was mortified. We made Dunster promise not to attack. She agreed, but she kept eyeing Digger like fresh meat.

Clancy reviewed the general plan, then made sure we all understood what our special duty was. Digger told Blackie to stay, but he wagged his tail and followed along. Digger apologized. He said it didn't matter anyway. Blackie would never cross the river. Then Dunster commanded Blackie to stay and he did.

As soon as we entered enemy territory, there was no talking or horsing around. Fortunately no one saw us. At the abutment, I felt a certain pride in showing Rudy and Dunster how to cross the bridge. On the other side, Clancy took the lead. We followed the path through the high weeds and soon heard shouting as we approached the trees.

Clancy stopped and faced us. "Okay," he whispered. "Everyone knows what they're supposed to do?" We all nodded.

"Let's move in closer." He motioned for us to follow. My heart pounded. I knew the plan would never work.

"Okay, get down," whispered Clancy.

I dropped, then pushed a stand of weeds aside. There they were. Naked bodies swarmed the slick embankment like mice on a block of cheese. I looked at Dunster. "Here's your chance," I whispered.

She was squinting behind her glasses, her tongue moved around wetting her lips. Finally, the ends of her mouth curled up and she smiled. It was broad, wicked.

"Is that all there is?" she whispered. She looked hard at Digger. He didn't answer. She reached over and punched him on the arm, then whispered louder. "Is that all there is?"

He rubbed his arm. "Yeah," he said, then turned away.

She looked like a cat that had just finished off a bowl of cream. Digger mumbled to himself.

Suddenly we heard Blackie barking in the distance. "Where did he come from?" whispered Grumble. Blackie shot past and didn't even see us. Digger called softly, but Blackie stopped for only a second before running on to the pond, still barking. We got a whiff as he passed. He smelled like the river.

"Shit," mumbled Digger. "Now what?"

Clancy looked over his shoulder. "Better go for it," he said.

Dunster hesitated for only a moment, then stood and ran toward the pond. The girl had courage. We followed close behind. Several swimmers spotted her and disappeared underwater. "Hi!" she shouted. Bare bodies stopped cold, darted back and forth, crashed into each other, slid down the bank, fell out of trees.

Dunster stood at the edge of the pond as the last two slipped into the water, trying to cover themselves. "Hi, Tom," she said. "What are you doing here?" One bobbing head attempted an answer but choked.

"And Steven, and Paul, I didn't expect to see you," she said. They were all guys from her class. We gathered beside her.

"Hi Pete," said Grumble. A half-submerged head nodded.

I whispered to Digger out of the corner of my mouth. "The firing squad there?"

"All of them," he said.

"Nice place you have here," said Dunster. She nodded and looked around. "Yep, maybe I'll just plop down here and read a book." No one spoke. She walked over to a log, sat down, adjusted her glasses, and opened her Nancy Drew mystery. "Don't let me interrupt," she said.

Clancy nodded, and everyone swung into action. Rudy and Mike quickly collected the guys' clothes, while Clancy and I gathered twigs and leaves for the fire Grumble was preparing. Dunster looked up occasionally to make sure there was no movement in the water. By the time everything was gathered, Grumble had a small fire lit. More limbs were added, and soon long fingers of flame crackled and popped, transforming Grumble's personality. Clearly he was a pyromaniac.

"Heave Ho!" shouted Mike. Shirts, shorts, socks, and underwear were heaved into the flames. We figured the shoes wouldn't burn.

"You're going to get killed!" came a voice from one of the faces, bobbing like apples. Then they fell into arguing among themselves. We were ready to run if they showed any inclination to come out, but they stayed low in the water. Teeth chattered. Lips turned blue. They didn't have a choice. The only place to come out was the embankment ten feet away from Dunster.

She made all the difference. She read and looked up and yawned. What an actress. Rudy was not as effective. Our prisoners argued about whether she was a girl.

"Digger!" shouted Dunster. She looked up smiling. "Sure would enjoy something nice to eat."

"So would I," said Digger. "But there isn't anything around." His mouth widened.

"Wrong," said Grumble. "There's an orchard on the other side of the pond." He continued staring into the flames.

"Well?" said Dunster.

"Do I have to?" said Digger.

"I'll go with you," I said.

We returned a short time later with a shirt loaded with pears. Everything looked the same, except that the soaking bodies, like frogs on a submerged log, were whiter, more wrinkled, swollen. Digger tossed three green pears toward Dunster.

She picked one up and took a bite without looking up. "Yuck," she said, then spit it out. "Thought you were going after apples?" She studied the small, green, worm-infested pear.

"There's only a pear orchard," I said.

"I don't like pears," she said. She wrinkled her nose and took a second bite. "Sometimes they give me a stomach ache."

"Tough," said Digger. He was smiling.

Dunster gave him a mean look, then returned to her reading. The pears were gone in a few minutes. Clancy and I tried one, but they were bitter. Finally Rudy threw a handful to the swimmers, and they converged like insects.

"Why did you do that?" said Digger.

"Because they needed something," she said.

"Oh yeah?" His face reddened. "Don't forget what they did to me." He pulled back the bandage and exposed the ugly, blue infection. All eyes were on him.

"Where did you get that?" said the redhead.

"The firing squad," said Digger. He flexed his calf muscle, making it look worse.

"Yuck," said the redhead and turned away.

"That's why we're here," said Clancy. "In case you

211

didn't know." He walked back to the log and sat down next to Dunster.

Rudy and I gathered around the fire while Grumble poked at the embers with loving care. An occasional curse was heard, but no effort was made to leave the water.

I was thinking about how we were going to get away when Dunster jumped up, looked in both directions, and ran suddenly into the bushes. It surprised me. Definitely not in the plan.

Even Grumble looked up from the fire. "Where did Dunster go?" There was mumbling in the pond.

"Don't know," mouthed Clancy. He looked worried, and I was ready to run for it. Clancy strolled over to the edge of the pond and looked down on the prisoners. "She'll be right back," he said. He clasped his hands and smiled. More chatter in the pond. Rudy and I pretended to collect more firewood, but the guys in the water knew we were stalling.

"Let's get 'em!" screamed the redhead.

"Wait!" shouted Digger. "Rudy here is also a girl." He pulled up Rudy's shirt, showing off her Pillsbury-labeled underpants.

No one made a move. Finally they howled and screamed and slapped the water like trapped animals, but they stayed in the water. We continued walking backward while Rudy held her ground. When we were a safe distance, Digger shouted. "Come on Rudy!" Curses exploded from the pond.

Rudy walked slowly backward, while Blackie ran back and forth in front of the water-logged, barking and snarling. When the redhead started out of the water, Rudy took off.

We reached the bridge in no time, then waited for Rudy to catch up. She arrived just as Dunster struggled out of the thicket. Her glasses were crooked, and she looked mad about something. "Where have you been?" said Grumble. "We could have been killed."

Dunster scowled at Grumble, then turned on Digger. "What was in those pears?" Digger shrugged, then grinned when she wasn't looking. He was beaming.

"What are we waiting for?" said Grumble.

Everyone scrambled up the bridge abutment, and Clancy tried to give Dunster a hand. "I'll do it myself," she snapped.

Grumble, Rudy, Clancy, and Mike moved easily across the steel beam, assisting each other at the point where the cross bracing was some distance apart. I led the second group with Dunster next and Digger bringing up the rear. I moved quickly across the open span, took hold of the diagonal brace, then turned and reached back for Dunster.

"I'm okay," she said, but I could tell she was nervous. It was the glasses—the bent frames. She took her first step out, wobbled, then caught herself. On her second step she sneezed, and this time lost her balance. She turned and started back, even reached out for Digger, but he wasn't there. He wasn't even close. She pitched forward, flaying the air.

Then hit with a splash. It wasn't a belly flop, but almost. And she disappeared for a moment. When she came up, screaming and kicking, she was covered with a black coat of muck. Her glasses were still on, but they were covered, and she splashed around blindly as if she were drowning. Finally she stood up. The water was waist deep.

"You okay?" I shouted.

She looked up. Her eyes looked like white holes in a bowling ball. "Where's Digger?" she screamed.

"She's okay," yelled Clancy.

"Yeah," whimpered Digger. He moved quickly across the open beam, crawled over me, then continued on to the abutment and leaped to the ground. He looked back only once, then disappeared into the thicket.

Blackie jumped into the water and swam out to Dunster, happy to have a companion for the crossing. He wanted to play, but Dunster would have none of it.

No one dared laugh. And Dunster wasn't talking on the way home. We kept our distance, upwind. Dunster walked with Blackie at her side. It was a perfect day.

TWENTY-EIGHT

For a few days we lived in fear of the gang from the south, but after they pelted Dunster's house with eggs and dismantled Grumble's go-cart, Clancy worked out a truce that brought the neighborhood wars to an end, at least until the following summer.

The only matter left unresolved was Dunster's violence against Digger. She was striking again with fanatic frequency. Digger's only consolation was the memory of that day at the bridge and also the gossip that Dunster's emergency trip into the brush resulted in a bad case of poison ivy in a most inconvenient place.

School started the day after Labor Day, which was less than a week away. Although I had forced it out of my mind all summer, I had to face it. But that week everything turned inside out.

It started in the middle of the night, when Mister Bean's Oldsmobile went through the rear of his garage. The crash awakened Mary Lou and me and she had to see what happened. We slipped out the back door, entered the moonlit yard, and ran to the alley only to find Clancy already there checking out the damage.

"Wake you up, too?" he said. He was in his pajamas.

The car's hood, shining in the moonlight, poked out of the rear wall of the garage. The grill and bumper looked undamaged, and the hood didn't even show a scratch.

"Where's Mister Bean?" I said.

"Went in just a minute ago," said Clancy.

"Bet he catches it from Mrs. Bean," said Mary Lou. "Dunster says he gets it all the time."

"What does she know?" I said.

"Dunster knows everything," she said.

Clancy grabbed my arm. "Listen!"

I heard voices off in the distance.

"Come on, let's go." He pulled me, and I dragged Mary Lou along. We ducked behind Clancy's fence.

"What's going on?" I whispered.

Clancy raised a finger to his lips. "Somebody's coming."

I heard a man talking, then saw three men through a crack in the fence. They wore dark suits and their white shirt fronts glowed in the moonlight. Whenever Mary Lou got nervous, she got the hiccups, and, sure enough, it happened. I slapped my hand over her mouth, but she pushed it away and handled it herself.

The men stopped for a moment and looked at the wreckage. "Jesus," whispered one of them. "So that's what made the noise."

"Goddam woman drivers," whispered another, shaking his head. They continued down the alley.

"How do you know it was a woman?" said the largest man, with a gruff voice.

Mary Lou hiccupped. I pushed her head down, and we hunkered even lower.

"What was that?" said the gruff man.

"I don't know," said another.

The gruff man walked to the fence. I could hear him breathing. He stood there too long. "Guess it was nothing," he said finally.

They started down the alley and I began breathing again. They continued talking, but they were too far away to hear. When we worked up enough courage to stand up and take a look, we barely saw them turn the corner.

"What was that all about?" I said.

"They came out of the Turk's gate," said Clancy.

"You sure?"

"I saw them."

"Shall we take a look?"

"Let's," said Clancy.

"I'm going home," said Mary Lou. Her voice quivered. "I'm tired." I was glad Mary Lou didn't want to go along. Too much to explain.

We found the Turk's gate open. "Holy shit!" said Clancy. "Look at that."

I was stunned. The entire yard was torn up, the

arbor and vines strewn about on the ground. Several shovels were left by whoever did the damage. It looked like a huge animal had gone berserk in search of food.

"Did those men do this?" I said.

"Yep," said Clancy.

"The Turk'll kill 'em when he sees this."

"But why would they do it?" Clancy picked up a shovel and pushed some vines aside. Every inch of ground had been dug up. "And where's the Turk?"

"Beats me," I said.

Clancy looked around. "Must've been mad about something."

"Or looking for the can."

"That's right, the can." He dropped the shovel and thought for a moment. "You know who they are, don't you?"

"Sure. The guys on the corner."

"Right. And the driver was one of 'em."

"You sure?"

"Yeah, it was him all right."

Clancy and I were tired and grumpy the following morning, but we told Digger and Rudy everything. Of course they had to go and see the yard. On the way, we passed the Beans' garage and had to stop to watch Mister Bean back his car out. One inch at a time. He didn't want to scratch the hood. Mrs. Bean was there giving orders. Digger made some smart remark and she asked us to leave.

When we arrived at the Turk's place, the gate was closed. We could hear men talking on the other side. Clancy took the hole in the fence, and Digger, Rudy, and I had to share the crack.

Two men, one in police uniform, walked back and forth, studying the damage. We couldn't hear what they were saying. We tried to get closer by going into the Beans' side yard, but Mrs. Bean was pruning rose bushes.

"Shit," said Digger. "Wouldn't you know it?" We returned to the fence, but the men had already gone.

"Something's fishy," said Clancy. "Where's the Turk?"

"Maybe inside?" I said.

"Doesn't make sense. And where was he last night?"

I entered the kitchen steeled for breakfast. My father was at the table, the paper spread out in front of him. His face was red, and he spoke louder than usual.

My mother leaned over his shoulder, reading. "It says his body was found last night on the railroad tracks south of town."

"Who's body?" I said.

My mother looked up. "The Turk's," she said.

The Turk? I dropped into a chair and looked at my hands. I couldn't believe it. "Is he dead?" I said, knowing what the answer would be. Mary Lou sat across from me taking it all in.

"Yes," said my father. "The police think he was murdered."

"Where does it say that?" said my mother.

"Right here." He pointed. She bent down and read again. Her pale gray face was almost buried in hair and curlers.

"Says the body was badly mutilated by a train, but there was little bleeding." She looked up. "What's that supposed to mean?"

"Read further. It says he was probably dead before the train hit him."

"Then he was murdered?" I said.

"I think so," he said. He glanced up. "Are you going to eat your breakfast?" He shook his head and looked out the window.

"Yes sir," I said, and took the first bite. The oatmeal was cold.

"I hope you don't know anything about this," he said.

"No, sir," I said. Mary Lou looked at me.

My father and mother continued talking, and I listened to everything they said. Finally, he kissed her and left for the office.

I was alone suddenly, thinking about the Turk and wondering what it was like to be dead. What happened to life? Where did it go? What did it feel like when it happened? I thought back to all the times I had seen him. The pool hall. The hobo village. His back yard. Then I thought about the men from the house on the corner. It had to be them. But they looked like ordinary men. Particularly the driver. He looked like my uncle. I couldn't believe he would kill anyone. It was confusing.

TWENTY-NINE

It was raining softly, but I knew everyone would be at the tree house. The umbrella of foliage above kept it dry. I liked the smell and sound of raindrops on wet leaves.

"Hear about the Turk?" said Digger the moment I came through the opening in the platform.

"My dad told me," I said, then sat down and leaned against the trunk. I was surprised he was the only one there.

"Think he was murdered?" said Digger.

"That's what the paper said."

"And those guys did it." He nodded toward the house on the corner, then wiped his nose with the inside of his wrist.

"Yahhhh!" screamed Clancy. He landed on the platform from the cable swing. I jumped back.

"Don't ever do that again," I said for the thousandth time. Clancy grinned like he'd done something wonderful.

"What do you think about the Turk?" said Digger.

Clancy's smile left. "He was murdered. And we

were there after it happened. When those guys were digging up the garden."

"You think they killed him right there?" I said.

"They did it somewhere. Then they put his body on the track." The thought was disturbing. That's all we talked about until Rudy arrived. Then we went to the pickle factory and the forest preserve even though it was still raining.

That night at dinner, my father said a policeman friend told him the murderer had already been arrested. "One of the bums from the village down by the tracks," he said. "The police figure he was after the Turk's money."

"Did the Turk have that much?" said my mother.

"Must have," he said. They talked about that for awhile, and all I could think about was what I was going to tell them. I had to tell someone.

"The bum didn't do it," I said.

My father looked at me.

I knew I was in trouble. "It was the men from the corner house. The men with the big black car."

His eyes narrowed. "How do you know that?"

I told him about going to the Beans' garage in the middle of the night, and the men who walked past after tearing up the Turk's garden. "Mary Lou was there," I said. "She can tell you."

Mary Lou just sat there and looked guilty.

"What was she doing there?" said my mother.

"Never mind," he said. "Did you see them, Mary

Lou?"

"I saw three men," she said. "But I don't know who they were."

He turned to me. "How do you know it was them?"

"Because they were the men who were in the Turk's house two weeks ago. I told you about that."

"Let's go through it one more time."

When I finished telling him everything, he walked into the living room and picked up the phone. I could hear him talking, and when he returned he said he'd talked to his policeman friend.

"Who else knows about this?" he said.

"Only Digger, Rudy, and Clancy."

"Don't tell anyone else," he said. His voice was soft. "And stay away from the Turk's back yard. And the house on the corner."

The kitchen was filled with the hopeful smell of burned oatmeal. Unfortunately, a fresh pan was cooking on the stove. The morning paper covered the table, and my father was still there.

"The police think it's either this guy or one of the other hobos," he said. "And that could be bad."

"Why?" said my mother.

"People are nervous about that encampment down by the switchyard. Remember the hobo accused of molesting a woman? The police had to break up a mob ready to tear the place apart. It wouldn't take much to trigger that."

"Was the fellow guilty?"

"He was released in a couple of days. But you know how people are."

My mother looked down at the paper again. There was a picture on the front page. "He doesn't look like a bad person," she said.

I walked around the table to get a better look. "Ernie!" I said. It was a large picture. Ernie was clean shaven. And his eyes looked sad.

"Ernest Fronds," said my Father. His eyes moved up to mine. "How did you know his name?"

"I don't know," I said. "I just . . ."

"You've been over there, haven't you?"

"Where?"

"The hobo village."

"A long time ago."

He looked off, shaking his head.

"He ate here once," I said. "Remember?"

"What are you talking about?"

"He raked our leaves." I looked at my mother. "Then you gave him a big dinner."

Her hands went to her mouth.

"Was it him?" said my father.

"The man had a beard." She looked closer at the picture. "It could have been him."

He turned back to me. "You're sure it was Ernest Fronds?"

"He's a friend of Clancy's," I said. "And he worked for the Turk."

225

"What did he do?"

"Took care of the grapes."

"I see." He leaned back in his chair. "Interesting." I thought I was going to catch it, but he just sat there thinking.

Everyone was talking up on the platform, and no one was listening. Finally Clancy stood up and held his ears. "Stop it!" he shouted. "We've got to take turns." He waited until the jabbering stopped. "And I'm first," he said.

"What do you mean?" I yelled.

More shouting.

Clancy stared me down. "It was Ernie's picture, right?"

"He's in jail," I said. "The police think he's the murderer. And my dad said people don't like the hobos living there. They might go after them."

"You mean the police?" said Clancy.

"No. Just people. He said a bunch of men tried to tear down the village once before, and the police had to stop them."

"Holy shit," said Clancy. He scratched his head. "That could happen again. Today. Now."

We looked at each other.

"What are we waiting for?" said Clancy.

In no time we were on the ground, running. I thought for only a second about the promise to my father. We raced across the highway then down the tree-lined street that led to the tracks. Clancy stopped at the end of the street when we heard men shouting. "Something's up!" he said.

He took off again, and we followed across three lines of empty tracks, then slipped under a box car, then another. As I came out from under the second, a gray, bearded man poked his head out of the car door, then ducked back in. He looked surprised, frightened. After two more boxcars, there was open track between us and the village. We stopped. A thin column of black smoke twisted skyward from the center of the huts. Tall weeds kept us from seeing any more. The voices grew louder.

"Better stay here!" shouted Clancy.

"Let's see what's going on," I said. I ran back to the nearest boxcar, crawled up the metal ladder, walked along the planking of the walkway, and sat down. In no time Digger and Rudy slipped in beside me. Clancy remained standing. We could see everything. The village, or what was left of it, was filled with men, like an army of giant ants. They were pushing down walls, tearing off roofs. A wood hut was on fire and scraps of wood and building materials were being thrown into the flames. A hut built of chunks of concrete was just a pile of rubble covered with pieces of corrugated roof. The shouting grew louder.

"It's awful," said Rudy.

"There won't be anything left," I said.

"Where are the hobos?" said Digger.

"Probably headed out of town," said Clancy.

"People just wanted to get rid of them," I said.

"My dad said they get blamed for everything," said Clancy.

I heard sirens in the distance, and in no time three police cars arrived. Policemen with billy clubs jumped out of the cars and the men scattered like rats fleeing a flood. Soon only the policemen were left. They tried to put out the fires. When the fire trucks arrived, all that was left was the smoking remains.

"Let's get out of here," said Clancy.

T H I R T Y

We climbed back up the monkey tree hot, tired. Everyone picked their favorite spot on the platform. Mine was at the edge where I could lean against the trunk.

"Pretty shitty," lisped Rudy.

"Yeah," said Clancy.

"Ernie's in jail," I said. "And the other poor guys are gone."

"And Ernie didn't do it," said Clancy.

"How could anyone kill someone?" said Rudy.

"Grumble and Mike hung a cat," I said.

"But that's different."

"Is it?"

"I'll bet it wasn't the driver," said Digger.

"He looks like my uncle," I said. "It couldn't have been him."

"Then which one did it?"

"Maybe all of them," said Clancy. We talked a long time about that.

I picked up an apple from the pile we'd swiped the day before and took a bite. It was sour all right. Then I saw the worm hole. I threw it over my shoulder, but it didn't make it to the edge. Rudy stood to kick it off. "Oh my gosh," she said.

"What?" said Digger. He turned his head and spit.

"Look," she said. She nodded toward the house across the street.

We crawled to the edge and looked down as the third police car pulled up and stopped. Patrolmen, carrying rifles, surrounded the house. Just like in the movies. Two more black Fords pulled into the driveway and six more men in suits got out. One carried a megaphone. Two of them walked around to see where the other cops were located, while the others talked.

We were all standing now. "They're gonna get those bastards," said Digger. He was beaming.

"What's he got that thing for?" said Rudy.

"It's a megaphone," said Clancy. "You'll see."

The man with the megaphone walked to the front of the house and shouted something through it. Although it was loud enough, we couldn't make out what he said. Three men walked to the front door and knocked, then waited for a long time. Finally the door opened.

"It's the driver," said Clancy.

"No it isn't," said Digger. He was squinting.

"Geez, you're blind," I said.

The driver walked out with his hands behind his head. Two policemen grabbed him, put him in handcuffs, and took him to a patrol car. The other three came out one at a time. They acted nervous. The police pushed them around. When all four were hand-cuffed and driven off, two of the men in suits went inside the house, while two others stood guard at the front door.

"Whew!" said Clancy. "Can you believe that?"

"I'll be damned," said Digger. I looked around and everyone had a big grin on their face. We watched until all the police cars had gone except two.

"Let's go home to lunch," said Clancy. "I'm dying." He grabbed the cable swing, stepped off, and swung down. He didn't let go at the bottom in order to swing up again, then dropped into a fresh pile of weeds, laughing. Digger was next on the cable, and I followed. I landed in the weed pile, rolled over, and watched Rudy descend like a giant bat. She landed and rolled into me. I sat up and smacked her on the arm. She laughed and punched me back.

That evening at dinner, my father filled us in on the details. I couldn't eat until I'd heard everything. He said that Ernie knew the Turk, and that the Turk gave food and clothing to the men in the village. In winter, he was their main source of support. It made no sense for anyone in the village to kill him. Of course, I knew all that.

But the Turk was involved in gambling, working as a bookie. The police figured the Turk wasn't paying enough kick-back, which was the motive for the murder. I told my father Clancy and I could help because of what we saw. He said he already mentioned it to his friend, and they wanted a statement from us, but the police already had more than enough for a conviction. I was disappointed.

On the front page the following morning was an exclusive on the murder with pictures of the four men who were captured. A small article with no picture described what had happened to the village. It also said that Ernest Fronds had been released. I took the front page to the monkey tree that morning and Clancy read all the articles out loud.

My father came home at lunch and said the police wanted to talk to Clancy and me. He took us both down to the police station where we met Clancy's father. He was much taller than my father, and he seemed serious. I liked Clancy's mother a lot better.

The police station was in the city hall—the only new building in town. My father thought it was too modern. We walked down a long corridor that smelled like fresh paint, then entered the office of the police chief. He was a thin, nervous man, and smoked a big cigar the whole time we were there. He tried to be nice.

Clancy did most of the talking, but I filled in every chance I got. A secretary took down everything we said. When we finished, the police chief thanked us for giving what he said was critical information, and we walked out feeling very important. On the way home, my father stopped at Dietrich's Ice Cream and bought us a cone.

It was still early in the afternoon when my father dropped us off at the monkey tree. Digger and Rudy were waiting. We told them everything, and they told us they saw Ernie walking down the alley past the Turk's place. Ernie told them he was headed out of town.

"Which way did he go?" said Clancy.

"Toward the tracks," said Rudy.

"Let's go and find him," I said.

"He'll be gone," said Digger. "He left a long time ago."

Clancy insisted on going anyway, and sure enough we found Ernie walking through the blackened remains of the huts. It was depressing. We stood some distance away waiting for him to notice. When he looked up, he walked over to us. He stopped for a moment and patted me on the shoulder, then walked on. I wanted to tell him we were sorry, but the time wasn't right. We watched him until he became a tiny spec in the lines of track. The hobos never returned to rebuild the village. And we never saw Ernie again.

I wasn't ready Tuesday morning following Labor Day. The day school began. I forced on new corduroy knickers and sharkskin-toed shoes from Marshall Fields. Everything felt stiff and miserable. "Aw shit," I mumbled.

"What was that?" shouted my mother from the kitchen. It was the day for ironing, and she'd already started.

"Nothing!" I shouted back.

"He said a bad word!" shouted Mary Lou. I walked

into the kitchen and found Mary Lou sitting there grinning. She liked everything about school, it fit her personality.

I looked into gray, throbbing oatmeal. It looked alive, like some strange organ. Here I was, about to enter the second grade for the second time. With a fresh new group of victims. Who could imagine how many insights, talents, natural abilities, would be drained off, dried up, lost in the wind. All in the name of education.

I was so depressed on the way to school, I didn't even look for Clancy or Digger. I wanted to be alone and brood on my misery. One thing I knew for sure, I was not going to play up to old Grizzly Bear. Someone had to carry on the work of Maxie Grover.

I was shocked when I saw Rudy waiting on the corner for her school bus. She wore a new blue dress and white anklets. She looked just like a girl.

I stopped for a moment, with no idea of what to say. I thought of that first day at the monkey tree when she was hanging upside down, showing off her Pillsbury labeled underpants. I still trusted her more than anyone.

"You look nice," I said.

Her face froze. "Aw, horse shit," she said. We stood looking at each other.

"See you later," I said.

"Yeah, see you."

I walked off, as a knot formed in my throat. When I

got far enough away, I cried. Why did it have to be that way? I loved Rudy. Not because she was a girl, but despite it. She was my friend. And I knew that things would never be the same.

Dunster moved away that fall, and we never saw her again. With Digger's new freedom, he started chumming around with older guys in his class. And, without Digger, I somehow lost my connection with Rudy. We moved in November. And even though it was only three blocks away, I seldom went to the park. I only saw Clancy at school, and I avoided everyone else from the year before. But I was no longer afraid of Old Grizz. I could read, spell, and add.

I was the oldest guy in class. No one dared say I flunked the second grade.